COUNTING COINS

A COZY QUILTS CLUB MYSTERY
BOOK 5

MARSHA DEFILIPPO

To get the latest information on new releases, excerpts and more, be sure to sign up for Marsha's newsletter.

https://marshadefilippo.com/newsletter

This book is dedicated to
The Wily Writers

CONTENTS

CHAPTER ONE: EVA

1

"Reuben, where are my keys?" Eva Perkins stood with her hands on her hips, glaring at the empty peg where they should have been, her voice tinged with frustration.

This would have been a rhetorical question for most people when addressing a cat, but Eva was expecting to get a reply. She discovered she could communicate with animals when she was a child and thought everyone had that ability. It didn't take long to learn that wasn't true, and it was safer for her to hide her talent. These days only a select few people knew of it.

She picked up the stack of mail she'd placed on her desk the day before, hoping she'd find the errant keys underneath it. With no joy there, she yanked out the center drawer where she kept her writing supplies, causing the contents to rattle as they shifted from their usual positions.

Reuben blinked his eyes, awakened from his morning nap by Eva's query and the racket she was making with her search. He yawned and stretched before replying.

How should I know? It's not as though I've used your keys. Ever. So, I have no idea. Why do you need them?

"I have an appointment at my attorney's office to draw up my Will."

Reuben's ears perked up and his eyes grew round.

You're not going to die, are you?

"Well, eventually, yes, but not anytime soon. You never know, though, so I want to have my paperwork in order, just in case. Here they are! I must have dropped them in my purse when I carried the groceries in yesterday and forgot to hang them on the peg." She fished the keychain out of one of the inside pockets and held it up victoriously.

Reuben was uncharacteristically quiet, catching Eva's attention and she looked in his direction. He was sitting upright in front of his cushion in the bay window staring off into space.

"Is something wrong?"

I'd never thought about what would happen to me if you died first until now. Who will take care of me, Eva?

Her jaw dropped and she stood motionless gawking back at him.

"I can't believe I hadn't thought of that. I've been so focused on what I should do about the house and my finances, that wasn't even on my radar. I'm so sorry. What would you think about going to live with Jim? The two of you seem to get along."

Jim Davis was Eva's significant other, although they didn't cohabitate.

Reuben looked up at the ceiling for so long that she thought he was ignoring her and was about to repeat the question.

I think I could tolerate him, but would I have to live in his house?

"Well, yes. I'm leaving this house to my nephew, Scott, but he may decide to sell it instead of moving in."

She had never had children of her own but Scott was her brother's son and he and his family were her closest living relatives.

Why aren't you giving it to me?

Eva rolled her eyes and let out a huff before turning back to her desk to pick up her purse and, with the keychain still in her hand, prepared to leave.

"I am not going to be one of those... I'll use the euphemism eccentric... people who put all of their property in a trust for their cats. You'll be fine with Jim or whoever else will take you if that becomes necessary. For now, I have to go or I'll be late for my appointment. We can talk about this when I get back." She waved her hand in his direction and walked out the door.

You can bet on it! he said, but she was already gone.

He climbed back on his cushion and watched as Eva's car backed out of the driveway and onto the road. He curled up on the pillow to resume the nap from which he'd been so rudely interrupted and fell asleep dreaming of ways to convince Eva he should continue to be the master of his domain.

2

Eva arrived at the offices of Mitchell & Johnson, Glen Lake's only law, office ten minutes later. Caleb Mitchell was the founder of the practice and its sole attorney when she first became a client twenty years prior. Fifteen years ago, he hired Dylan Johnson after he'd passed his bar exam and in only two years with the firm, made him a senior partner. Their personalities were polar opposites. Caleb was old-school New England, no nonsense and down to business whereas Dylan was extroverted and congenial.

Eva parked her car in the expanded driveway and admired the building's facade. The offices were located in a converted two-story Queen Anne Victorian style home on the Hudson Road. A ramp had been added to one side of the entry to make it wheelchair accessible but otherwise the exterior looked much as it must have when it was erected in the late 1800s. The clapboard siding was painted a crisp white and many of the upper windows on the first floor and the front door had the original stained glass. Stately maple trees that were planted as saplings when the house was first built had survived the harsh winter conditions of New England and now towered over the roof providing shade in the summer.

A bell chimed announcing her arrival when Eva opened the door and stepped into the foyer. A brass umbrella stand was partially hidden behind a Ficus tree tucked in the corner. There was a staircase which led up to the offices of Grace Foster, the firm's paralegal and Kyle Mitchell, Caleb's son, who was the office manager. Amber Hayes, who served as the personal assistant to Caleb and Dylan, appeared from her office to the right of the entry that had been the formal parlor when it was a residence. She guessed Amber was in her late thirties or possibly early forties and had been with Mitchell & Johnson for as long as she could remember. She was always impeccably put together and today was no exception.

That's exactly how I would like to have dressed when I was her age and had her figure, Eva thought, admiring Amber's black woolen slacks and cream-colored long-sleeved turtleneck sweater, accented with a floral scarf in shades of blue that matched the color of her eyes and complemented her short dark hair.

"Ms. Perkins, how nice to see you again. We have your documents set up in the conference room. If you would just follow me, and I'll let Mr. Mitchell know you're here."

She led the way down the hallway to the right of the staircase and into the former dining room. The furnishings were reminiscent of its original purpose, with its long rectangular table centered in the middle of the room, flanked by chairs on either side and at the ends. Arranged at the head of the table were a manilla folder which Eva assumed contained the copies of her Will, along with a yellow legal pad and two pens. She took a seat perpendicular to it, facing the door, knowing intuitively the chair in front of the folder was for Caleb.

"Would you like a cup of coffee or tea, or perhaps a glass of water?" Amber asked.

"No, thank you. I'm fine."

"Mr. Mitchell should be right in." Amber slid the pocket door closed behind her.

Eva had been in the conference room before but on this occasion, having no one else to distract her, she took more time to inspect its décor. The built-in cabinets in two corners of the room were filled with books now rather than fine china dinnerware, and inside the doors and drawers of the buffet table were office supplies instead of linens, serving dishes, and silverware. A concession to its former purpose, a sterling silver coffee pot sat on a silver tray that Eva thought might be used for conferences when more people were in attendance. Another set of closed pocket doors took up a section of the wall at the far end of the room. *That must go into the old kitchen. They probably use it as a break room,* she thought. The sound of the door which Amber had departed from sliding back into its slot interrupted her reverie, and Caleb Mitchell entered the room with his hand outstretched.

"Good morning, Eva. How nice to see you again."

Eva extended her hand to his.

"It's nice to see you, too, Caleb." Their close proximity in age and having known him for twenty-plus years gave her the confidence to address him so casually. Otherwise, his stern demeanor would have solicited the more formal greeting of Mr. Mitchell. His record of service to the community softened his reputation for coming across as a grumpy old man. Once you got past the crusty exterior, Caleb had a kind, giving side and a dry sense of humor.

"Have you had a chance to read through the documents already?"

"Yes, Amber sent me the drafts, and everything appears to be in order. Something occurred to me just this morning, though. I don't know if it would necessitate a change to the Will, but if I should die before my cat, Reuben, would a simple verbal agreement with someone to take care of him be enough? Or would I need to have a written document in place?"

"Do you have someone in mind?"

"I do, but I haven't discussed it with him yet. As I said, I only thought of it this morning." *But I wouldn't have if Reuben hadn't brought it up*, she thought, somewhat ashamed that she hadn't on her own.

"I would think a verbal agreement would be sufficient, but it would increase the chances your wishes are honored if you put something in writing on your own and give it to the executor of your estate for safekeeping."

"That's a good idea. I'll do that."

"In that case, I'll let Amber know we're ready to sign the documents." He left the room and returned with her following behind.

"Grace and Kyle will be right down and we can get these finalized," Caleb said. As if on cue, Eva heard the sound of footsteps coming down the stairway.

Grace Foster was dressed in a navy-blue pantsuit and white silk blouse and her necklace and earrings were a simple, but timeless, design. Her honey blonde hair was cut in a flattering chin-length style and her manicured fingernails were a soft shade of pink. Everything about her exuded understated elegance and Eva wondered if Caleb insisted on a dress code.

Kyle had inherited his father's tall, lean build, but his features had none of Caleb's sharp angles. Eva had met Kyle's mother, Louise, at a community fundraiser a year earlier, shortly before she died. She was the obvious choice for who Kyle resembled. As Eva watched him enter the room, she sensed an undercurrent of tension in his usually relaxed personality but didn't have time to reflect on it. Caleb had already called the meeting to order with instructions for Eva to initial the bottom of every page and add her full signature on the line above her printed name on the last one. When she had done as instructed, he slid the document to Amber, who initialed each page and signed as the witness and then passed it along to Kyle, who did the same.

"Do you state that you are of sound mind and body and have signed this document of your own free will?" Grace asked, and when Eva replied affirmatively, Grace signed the document in her capacity as a notary public and added her official notary seal.

"That should do it," Caleb announced. "Would you like us to hold the original for you here or take it with you? Amber will make a copy of the executed Will to take with you for your records or we'll keep a copy here if you take the original."

"I'll take the original with me to put in my safe deposit box. My nephew is a signatory on the account, so will be able to access it when I die. I've let him know he should also get in touch with you. I bought one of those workbooks called *I'm Dead. Now What?* that I've filled out, and plan to keep it in the safe deposit box along with the Will." Eva said.

Caleb chuckled. "I've heard of those and wish all my clients were as organized. It makes things so much easier for everyone and as the executor of your Will, I'm sure he'll appreciate your forethought. Amber, would you please make a copy of the Will for our records?"

"Of course. I'll be right back."

"It was very nice to see you again, Ms. Perkins." Kyle smiled at her before turning to his father. "Unless you need me for something else, I should go back to my office. I was in the middle of a project and should go back to work on it."

Caleb frowned at Kyle with an irritated glance, which he quickly hid behind a neutral expression.

"You're free to go. We shouldn't require you for anything further," his tone was even, but Eva detected that same undercurrent of strain between the two men that she'd experienced earlier.

"I should probably go back to my office, too. It was a pleasure, as always, to see you." Grace smiled at Eva and extended her hand.

"Thank you. You, as well," she said and turned to Caleb. "If my significant other is agreeable, I'll see if the workbook has a category for what to do about pets and make sure that's filled out for my nephew, too. If it does, I must have skipped right past it."

"Perfect," Caleb replied. "In that case, we're done for today as soon as Amber makes the photocopy, but if you need anything else, you know where to find us." Caleb gave her one of his rare smiles, but Eva didn't think it was disingenuous.

No sooner had he spoken than Amber returned and placed the documents in a manilla envelope and handed them to Eva; then waited for her to gather her things and walked with her to the door.

"Eva, what a nice surprise!"

She turned at the sound of Dylan Johnson's voice. She couldn't help but return his warm smile as she spotted him coming down the hallway from his office at the back of the building.

"It's good to see you, too, Dylan. That was quite the get-together last week!"

Eva and Jim had been invited as guests of Jim's son, Christopher, who was Dylan's neighbor.

"It was a good turnout. I'm glad Chris brought you and Jim along," Dylan said.

"Me, too. I hope to see you again soon," she said, not realizing how that sentiment would come to pass.

CHAPTER TWO: KYLE

1

Kyle struggled to concentrate on the monthly balance sheet he'd been working on for the firm when he'd been summoned to witness Eva Perkins's Will. Tallying the income and expenses reminded him of his personal finances. He made a good salary, but he was living beyond his means and his wife, Erica, spent money as though they had a money tree growing in their back yard. He tried, but she was a master at manipulation and putting up with the tears and pouting for days after any conversation aimed at reining in her spending wasn't worth it. But now the situation had reached critical mass. The delinquent account notices were piling up, and he would soon be two months behind on their first and second mortgages. It was only this sense of desperation, and not having any other options, that he made the decision to approach his father for a short-term loan to bring everything up to current status. Their relationship had always been difficult, and Caleb's strict parenting style had not been offset by expressions of affection. Any emotional warmth he'd received came from his mother, but when that happened, Caleb accused her of coddling him. Kyle never felt as though he measured up to Caleb's expectations. To make matters worse, he treated Dylan like the son he'd always hoped to have, and Kyle was his disappointment. It wasn't Dylan's fault, but still, he had resented him since Dylan first came to the firm as a law clerk. To rub even more salt in the wound, Caleb had promoted Dylan as a full partner within only two years of joining the practice and his salary was nearly double that of Kyle's. It wasn't fair. If he was making that much money, he wouldn't be in the mess he was in now.

Kyle glanced at the time. Not long now. He'd rehearsed his speech and as soon as the office closed for the day and the two of them were alone, he would ask for the loan. His stomach knotted at the thought of how Caleb would react, but he had no choice. He jumped when Grace stuck her head in the doorway to say goodnight and pasted a smile on his face to return the farewell. He waited another five minutes, listening for any sounds indicating Dylan and Amber had left before making his way downstairs, using the back stairs that would take him next to Dylan's office and the hallway leading toward the front of the building. Dylan's office was empty, so he made his way forward, checking the break room and conference room along the way. When he reached her office, Amber was putting on her coat, preparing to leave.

"Is Dylan still here?" he asked.

"You just missed him. You might be able to catch him in the parking lot," Amber replied.

"That's okay. I'll catch up with him tomorrow. It's not important. You have a good night and I'll see you tomorrow."

"Thanks! You, too," she said and continued on her way.

He waited until he heard her car exit the driveway and took a deep breath, steeling himself to approach Caleb. He knocked before opening the door. Caleb looked up, an annoyed expression on his face at being interrupted. He laid his pen on the desk, leaned back in his chair, and folded his hands across his stomach, waiting for Kyle to state his reason for disturbing him.

"Do you have a minute?" Kyle asked, keeping his tone light.

"Not really, but you're here. What do you want?" Caleb gestured with his hand for Kyle to sit in one of the chairs in front of his desk and then folded them in his lap again.

This was going to be even harder than he'd expected, if that was possible. Caleb's brusque response had him waffling about continuing with his request. Sitting in a chair as he'd been instructed, he cleared his throat, more as a delaying tactic to booster his courage, before beginning.

"I'm having some cash flow problems... it's just temporary... but I need to borrow twenty thousand dollars to catch up. I'm not asking you to give it to me; it would be a loan. I'll set it up with our payroll vendor so it's on them to make sure it's taken out of my paycheck..." Kyle's voice trailed off. He had rehearsed more, but the look on Caleb's face told him his words would be wasted.

"What's to keep you from coming back to me at the end of the month, begging for another twenty thousand? Do you plan to cut up your credit cards so your wife will stop shopping?"

The words stung. Kyle understood the message underneath them. *You can't manage your wife or your money. You're not a good risk for a loan.* The bankers he'd spoken with hadn't worded their denials in exactly the same way, but they came down to the same thing. He felt a flush in his cheeks begin to rise.

"If that's what it will take for you to approve a loan, then yes, I'll do that."

Caleb scoffed. "Even if you did, I would still say no. You need to learn to manage your money. If that means you have to declare bankruptcy, then so be it. I'm not going to enable your poor judgement. You're a business manager, Kyle. Act like one and figure this out, but I'm not your personal banker."

All the nervousness Kyle had felt when he started his request shifted. His jaw tightened, and he clenched his hands until his knuckles turned white. The two men faced off in a staring contest until Kyle leaped up and began pacing the office, trying to blow off his anger.

"Why can't you be more like Dylan?"

That was the final insult. In frustration and a place of deep emotional hurt, Kyle picked up a glass paperweight from the credenza and juggled it in his hands. In this state of blind fury, he turned and hurled it toward the bookcases behind Caleb's desk. His back had been toward Caleb while he paced, so he wasn't aware he'd risen out of his chair. He'd intended for the paperweight to launch high and to the right of where Caleb was sitting. Instead, it hit him squarely on his left temple with a sickening crack. Caleb's eyes were filled with surprise when they briefly met Kyle's and then rolled up as his body collapsed to the floor. Kyle's mouth gaped in shock and disbelief, and he stood rooted to the floor as his mind processed what had just happened. What seemed like minutes but was only seconds later, the trance broke and he rushed to his father's side. He knew he wouldn't find a pulse, but checked anyway. His fears were confirmed and panic overtook him.

"It was an accident. I didn't mean to hit you. I was aiming for the bookcase."

Despite knowing his father couldn't hear him, Kyle was compelled to say the words aloud. He reached into his jacket pocket with the intention of retrieving his phone to call 911, but stopped as an internal dialogue began.

Make it look like a break-in. Pick up the paperweight and hide it somewhere, a voice in his head instructed, and he reached out to pick it up, but then paused. *No, just wipe it off so your fingerprints aren't on it and put it back.* He hesitated, unsure of which advice to follow before deciding to take it with him. It was glass. He could smash it up and toss the pieces some place where no one would think to search for them.

If he was going to make the police believe this was a break-in, he would have to damage the back door. *How did they do that on crime shows?* He'd need something like a crowbar, wouldn't he?

He thought about the toolbox stored in the filing room for the occasions when they needed a minor repair, but knew he wouldn't find one in it. Maybe a screwdriver would work instead, though. And he needed some paper towels to pick up the paperweight.

Lock the door! You don't want anyone to find you here.

It was unlikely someone would be coming to the office at this time of night, not even one of the staff, but it sounded like good advice. Kyle went to the front door and secured the deadbolt.

Having a purpose and a plan settled his nerves. He found the toolbox and snatched the biggest flathead screwdriver in it before replacing the toolbox in its usual spot. He grabbed the roll of paper towels from the break room and left the screwdriver to use when he got back from Caleb's office. The silence of the building was unsettling, and a chill went up his spine. *Get a grip on yourself!* he admonished and set to his tasks. After wrapping the paperweight in several layers of paper towels and putting it in his pocket, he closed Caleb's door, and returned the roll to the break room and then went to his office to find his keys. Once out the back door, he locked it and then realized he didn't have the screwdriver. Letting out his breath in a huff of disgust, he unlocked the door and retrieved it from the table where he'd left it. With the door once again locked, he inserted the screwdriver into the space between the frame and the door. It took a few tries, and he made sure to damage the frame to convince the police it had been a break-in. He wiped the head of the screwdriver on his pants in case there were any fragments of wood on it and returned it to the toolbox. He wasn't worried about fingerprints. His prints *should* be on the handle and it would be more suspicious if they weren't. Satisfied he'd covered his tracks, he went to his car, which he'd parked at this end of the parking lot when he'd arrived that morning. He still didn't have the money, but perhaps he could work something out with his creditors to wait just a little longer. After all, he'd have his inheritance coming, and he'd talk to Dylan about giving him a raise once things settled down. The heaviness of the paperweight in his pocket broke through his subconscious and his optimistic mood vanished. *As long as you can get away with it,* the voice reminded him.

2

Kyle stared at his reflection in the bathroom mirror. His puffy eyes told the story of his sleepless night. Every time he closed his eyes, he saw the image of his father's lifeless body. He turned on the cold water, scooped it into his hands, and splashed it onto his face. After drying it with the hand towel that hung on a rod next to the sink, he checked his face again. He didn't look any better, but the frigid water against his skin had revived him.

You're going to have to act normal. When they tell you he's dead, you'll have to react as though you're in shock. You don't have to break down in tears, but you need to at least come across like a grieving son.

He nodded his head at his reflection as though acknowledging the advice and felt a sense of confidence returning now that he had a plan for the day. It was going to be a long one. He couldn't be sure who would be the first one to open the office, but on any other day, it would be either him or Amber. Occasionally, Dylan or Grace arrived early to get a head start on their day, especially if they had a pending court case. He'd need an excuse for not arriving sooner, but he didn't want to be the first one on the scene. It was already bad enough that he was the last one to leave which might put him in the crosshairs.

He caught his breath as he realized he needed an alibi. Erica hadn't said anything to him about when he'd gotten home, so he was safe on that score if the police questioned her. It wouldn't have been the first time he'd been late coming home from the office and he doubted she'd even noticed.

You can say you worked late to finish the balance sheet.

How late, though? He thought back to when he left the office. *Why didn't I think to check the time?* he scolded himself. *Take a breath. Just think, and count backwards from how long it took you to clean up and how long you talked to Dad. Take about five or ten minutes off from that and it should be close enough. It's not like they can be exact about the time of death and no one saw you leave.*

He stepped into the shower and let the hot water stream over him to relax the tension in his body. Twenty minutes later he turned off the water and finished the rest of his morning routine and went to the kitchen. Erica was in the mudroom getting the kids into their jackets to wait for the school bus. Their daughter, Peyton, was ten years old and their son, Zach, was eight, so perfectly capable of putting on their own jackets, but not always as quickly as was needed to get to the bus stop before the bus arrived. That would mean Erica would have to drive them to school and despite being a stay-at-home-mom, she always grumbled about not having the time to do it. On those occasions when it did happen, Kyle thought of mentioning that if she took away their iPads in the morning, they would probably get ready faster. In the end, he put that in the choose your battles category and kept quiet.

Kyle walked over to give each of them a kiss. "Did you get your homework done?"

"Yes, Dad," Peyton and Zach answered, their voices reflecting the undisguised annoyance of being asked this every school morning.

"Alright, have fun, be kind, and learn things."

They rolled their eyes. This was the same thing he also said to them every morning before they headed out the door.

"I'll be back in as soon as the bus comes. You were late coming down, so I didn't make you any eggs, but there's coffee and muffins if you're hungry," Erica said over her shoulder as she followed Zach and Peyton out the door.

Kyle checked his watch to see how much time he needed to delay before leaving. It was seven-thirty and it would take him twenty minutes to drive to the office. Amber would be in the office at eight to make sure everything was ready before any clients arrived at eight-thirty. He'd have time for the coffee and a muffin. He took a plate from the recently installed kitchen cabinets and walked to the coffee bar which had been added as part of the renovation, to fill his mug and returned to the island, also newly installed. Erica had insisted the granite countertops that had only been in place three years needed to be replaced with quartz. The kitchen renovation with its new cabinets, countertops, and top of the line appliances had cost close to a hundred thousand dollars, which meant putting an equity loan on the house. Kyle had to admit it turned out like something from a magazine, but there hadn't been anything wrong with the old kitchen. The extra loan payment had stretched their budget to the max, and he'd been surprised the bank had even approved it. He'd hoped they wouldn't, so he didn't have to be the one for Erica to blame because it couldn't happen. She wasn't pleasant to be around when she didn't get her way. Her parents had spoiled her all her life and expected him to do the same. Trying to talk to her about not spending so much money was a lesson in futility.

His face lit up as he took another bite of the muffin and had a flash of inspiration. *I can stop by The Checkout and pick up a box of doughnuts to explain why I wasn't already there right at eight o'clock.* He put the last bite in his mouth and carried the dishes to the dishwasher. He was putting on his coat when Erica came back in.

"Have to leave now. The muffins gave me the idea to pick up some muffins or doughnuts for the office. I'll see you tonight." He kissed her on the cheek and left before she had time to even say goodbye.

3

When Kyle arrived at the office, he saw an ambulance and

police car parked in the driveway. He drove to the back entrance, parked his car in its space at the rear of the building and then pulled the visor down to slide the mirror compartment door aside. He arranged his face in an appearance of concern, and satisfied that it was convincing, rushed to the front of the building where the first responders were gathered, remembering to bring with him the box of doughnuts he'd bought at The Checkout. Amber was sitting in the back of the ambulance, sobbing hysterically, and one of the EMTs was speaking to her in a soothing tone of voice in an attempt to calm her.

"What's going on?" Kyle asked, looking at the group gathered around the ambulance and addressing all of them rather than anyone in particular.

A uniformed sheriff approached Kyle, holding up his hand to stop him as he began to walk toward Amber. "I'm Deputy Tremblay. And you are?"

"I'm Kyle Mitchell. I work here. What's going on?" he asked again.

"Mitchell. Are you related to Caleb Mitchell?"

"Yes, I'm his son. For the third time, would you please tell me what is going on here? Is something wrong with Amber?" This time he added an angry edge to his voice.

"I'm sorry to have to inform you, Mr. Mitchell, that your father is deceased. Ms. Hayes found him in his office when she arrived this morning."

"Dead? That can't be possible. I want to see him." Kyle attempted to walk around Deputy Tremblay but he caught Kyle's arm, the one not holding the doughnuts, to stop him from entering the building.

"You can't go in there now. We're waiting for a state police officer and crime unit to arrive and we can't contaminate the scene."

Kyle turned to regard Deputy Tremblay with a confused expression. "What do you mean, it's a crime scene? Was he murdered?" He hoped his voice carried an appropriate amount of incredulity. "Amber, what is he talking about?"

The EMT's efforts must have worked. Amber was no longer sobbing, but she still looked shaken.

"As soon as I walked in the front door, I noticed the alarm system hadn't been set and the office felt colder than usual and then I noticed the back door wasn't completely shut. There weren't any other cars in the parking lot and I knew the last person leaving would have checked all the doors last night. There was no way your father would have left the door open when he got here this morning so I thought we must have been broken into. I started checking the offices to see if computers were missing. I figured that's what thieves would be looking for. Everything was where it should be in Dylan's office so I came back to mine and then went to your father's office. The door was closed, but I didn't hear anything so I went in…" Her chin began to quiver and her eyes started to water but she straightened her shoulders and pressed her lips into a thin line until she was composed enough to continue. "He was lying there on the floor and I could tell he was dead. I called 911 right away but then I lost it, and I couldn't stop crying or I would have called you, too. I knew you'd be coming in and it was important to call the police first. I hope you're not mad at me."

Kyle felt his heart tighten when he saw her face. He was responsible for what she was going through but his sense of self-preservation kicked in. He had no choice but to keep up the ruse.

"Of course not. You did the right thing." He looked down at the box of doughnuts. "Is it okay if I put these in the break room?"

Deputy Tremblay didn't hesitate before replying, "No, in fact, you and Ms. Hayes will have to remain outside of the building so the mobile crime unit can investigate the scene. The entire building will be inspected, not just your father's office."

Before Kyle had a chance to respond, Dylan arrived with

Grace right behind him, both wearing an expression of confusion and concern.

"What's going on?" Dylan was the first to speak, repeating the same question Kyle had asked.

"It's Dad; he's dead. Amber found him when she opened up this morning," Kyle replied, keeping his voice even. "This is Deputy Tremblay. We're waiting now for someone from the State Police to show up to investigate. It looks like it was murder."

Grace gasped upon hearing the words.

Kyle turned to Amber, assuming a take-charge attitude. He was the office manager, after all.

"We're going to have to close the office today… no, make it for the rest of the week. You'll need to call all the clients who have appointments to reschedule." He turned to Dylan. "Will you be able to take over for Dad's clients?"

"I think so, at least temporarily. I'll need some time to go through their files to get acquainted with their situations. We'll need to talk about what happens long term, though. Depending on the caseload and complexity of their situations, we might have to hire another lawyer. Grace, you might be able to take some of them. Once I've had a chance to review them, I'll pull out the ones I think you can take over."

She nodded her acknowledgement before turning to Amber. "Do you need some help making the cancellations?"

"That would be great. I have the calendar on my laptop in my purse. It's a good thing I thought to bring it out with me." She glanced down at the purse sitting beside her. "What should we tell them?" she asked Kyle.

Before Kyle could answer, Dylan cut in. "Tell them we've had an emergency come up that requires us to close the office temporarily and we'll be back in touch next week to reschedule. Apologize for the inconvenience, but if anyone asks for more information, tell them we'll explain after we've had time to deal with the emergency and that's all we can say for now. Although once word gets out that the office is blocked off by crime scene tape, it won't take long for the rumor mill to start."

"Okay. I'll start on that as soon as we get back inside. I'll go through Caleb's appointments and Grace, why don't you start with yours and Dylan's? All the contact information is in the scheduler program," Amber said.

Kyle stayed quiet, but inside he was fuming. He should have been the one to instruct Amber about what to do. He was the Office Manager, after all. Did Dylan think he wasn't capable of figuring that out? *Typical Dylan. He treats me just like Dad did. As though I don't have a brain in my head.* One more thing to add to the list of reasons why he resented Dylan.

"How long will it take for the crime unit to clear the scene? We can't just stand around here in the driveway and, as you just heard, we need to let our clients know they shouldn't come to the office. Some of them may already be on their way. What if we used the conference room?" Kyle said to Deputy Tremblay.

"As I already stated, the entire building is off limits until they've completed their investigation. That could be later today or even days later, depending on how much of the building they need to look through and what they find," Deputy Tremblay answered, his voice even but with an air of authority that told Kyle there was no point trying to sway him.

The sound of a van turning into the driveway drew everyone's attention toward the road. Lettered on its side were the words Maine State Police Evidence Response Team. A man emerged from the van carrying what looked like a large toolbox and sought out Deputy Tremblay. "Deputy Tremblay? I'm Ian Nelson. I'm here to investigate the report of a homicide."

After introductions were made, Ian Nelson and Deputy Tremblay left to begin their work inside.

"Where should we go now?" Amber asked.

"Can we go to Caleb's house?" Dylan asked Kyle.

Caleb lived next door to the office. It was the house Kyle had grown up in and would now be his, he realized. Caleb had originally used the front parlor of the house as his law office until the practice had outgrown the space. When the house next door came on the market, he bought it both for its convenience and the price. It hadn't been maintained well over the years but he would need to renovate the rooms anyway so that hadn't discouraged him.

Kyle hesitated, looking at the ground as he mentally went through the rooms from the perspective of the best place for each of them to set up their temporary offices. He looked up to find three expectant faces waiting patiently for his response.

"That's a great idea, Dylan." He hoped the smile he arranged on his face appeared sincere. Leave it to Dylan to think of what he should have suggested as soon as Deputy Tremblay told them they couldn't use the office. "There should be room for everyone to spread out and I think the internet connection should be able to handle everyone using it at the same time. Just don't expect it to be fast with that many people sharing the line. Follow me."

He led them through the path leading from the driveway of the office to the house, unlocked the door, and disarmed the security system.

"I brought doughnuts in case anyone's interested. I'll put them in the kitchen and make a pot of coffee," Kyle said, holding up the box for them to see and then walked to the kitchen with the others trailing behind him. He set the box down in the center of the table, but no one took him up on the offer.

"I'll use my dad's office. I don't have my laptop with me so I'll need to use his computer. There's space in the den, the dining room, and the living room. You can each decide who wants to be where."

"Ladies first," Dylan said, smiling.

"Why don't you take the den?" Grace suggested to Dylan. "If it's okay with you, Amber, I'll set up in the dining room. I need to spread out the paperwork I brought home to work on and it would be easier to do that on the table in there."

"Sure, I'm okay with that. I'll mostly be making phone calls so I don't need anything more than my laptop and a place to sit. Is there a printer I can use to print out the contact info for the calls Grace needs to make?"

"Sure, Dad has one in his office that's Bluetooth enabled. Why don't we do that now?"

Amber followed him into Caleb's office and they set up her computer to sync with the printer. Kyle turned on the machine and it began its warmup sequence while Amber located the file Grace needed to make her calls and entered the print commands. Kyle waited for it to spit out the document. He frowned as his hand shook slightly when he picked up the sheet of paper.

Don't worry about that. She won't think twice if she saw your hands shaking. You just found out your father was murdered, remember? It would be worse if they thought you were acting like nothing happened.

"Thanks, Kyle. We'll get right on making the calls. It's lucky… and kind of spooky, that no one had clients coming in until ten o'clock. It's almost like…" Her voice trailed off as she realized what she was about to say and to whom. "Sorry," she muttered and hustled out of the room, her cheeks a pale shade of pink.

Kyle turned on Caleb's desktop computer. His father hadn't been as security conscious at his home office and even if he had, Kyle had figured out the password when Caleb was away at a Bar convention. His father didn't need to know that.

It suddenly occurred to him he hadn't called Erica to tell her about Caleb. With all the distractions of the past half hour, it had slipped his mind. He braced himself for the conversation, rehearsing lines in case anyone overheard, when it hit him. *I'm going to need to make arrangements for the funeral. Don't forget about the life insurance policy. I'll need to file a claim. And the Will. Dylan will probably be able to fill me in about that. The most logical place to find it will be in the safe at Dad's house, though, so I might not even need Dylan's help. Not much longer and my money problems will be solved.* His lips twitched as he fought the urge to smile.

Dylan walked past Caleb's office on his way to the kitchen for coffee and a doughnut. He glanced in the open doorway and observed Kyle so deep in thought, he didn't notice him passing by. He thought he must be mistaken when he glimpsed Kyle's expression change. *Is Kyle smiling?* It had been fleeting, but he could have sworn that was a smile. He blinked before looking again to double-check what he thought he saw, but Kyle wasn't smiling now. *Must have been your imagination*, he thought as he shook his head in disbelief and continued walking to the kitchen, but the uneasy sensation remained in the back of his mind.

4

An hour later, Dylan was still working in the den and Amber and Grace had finished their calls to clients, avoiding revealing the true cause for the cancellations despite the attempts of several of them pushing for more details. Ian Nelson had been there earlier and taken Kyle's and Amber's fingerprints for elimination of any found by the investigators. Dylan's and Grace's prints were already on file.

Kyle had called Erica, but the call went straight to voicemail. He left a message asking her to call back as he had urgent news but didn't want to explain in a voicemail. She still hadn't returned his call.

He didn't want any evidence of his To Do list on Caleb's computer and without his laptop, he'd had to resort to taking a new legal pad from one of the drawers in Caleb's desk to start it. He'd speak with Dylan later about the Will when they were alone. The doorbell rang, interrupting his thoughts. He walked to the door, a scowl on his face. He opened it to find Deputy Tremblay accompanied by two men in suits.

"I'm sorry to interrupt, but I'd like to introduce you to Detectives Smith and Roberts. They'll be handling the investigation into Mr. Mitchell's death," Deputy Tremblay gestured to the respective detective as he announced their names.

Kyle's stomach knotted. He hadn't been asked yet to give an account of his whereabouts. In his head, he had role-played various scenarios to rehearse answers to the questions he expected to be asked. He felt confident he could bluff his way through this, but a tiny sliver of doubt lingered that had his nerves on edge.

"Of course, come in. I'll get the others."

"That's okay. It would be best if we interviewed you separately first," the one Tremblay had introduced as Roberts said. He spoke to the one named Smith. "Why don't we split up and each take two of the staff?"

"Sounds like a plan. Where will we find the others?" Smith asked Kyle.

"Dylan is in the den and Grace should be in the dining room. Amber was in the living room earlier. Follow me and I'll take you to Dylan."

"That's okay. I think Deputy Tremblay and I can figure it out. You can give your statement to Detective Roberts."

"Oh, of course. I'm working in here," he said, and led Roberts into Caleb's office.

"Who was the last one to leave the office yesterday?" the detective asked once they were seated and he had removed a small notebook and pen from the inside pocket of his jacket.

"My father was the only one in the office when I left," Kyle answered, meeting the detective's eyes and keeping his voice level just as he'd practiced. "Caleb Mitchell was my father."

"And you work for him?" Roberts asked.

"Yes, I'm the Office Manager."

"The office has a security system. Did you set the alarm before you left?"

"No. I knew my father would do that when he left."

"Do you know of anyone who would want to harm your father?" Roberts asked, looking up from his notes.

The detective's eyes met Kyle's, making him want to squirm in his seat. Using every ounce of strength he had, he forced himself to keep his face composed, but out of sight of the detective, his hands were clenched together in his lap.

"No, I don't. He stopped doing criminal cases when Dylan Johnson joined the firm. His practice is... was... mostly estate planning and setting up corporations these days. I can't imagine any client who would have a reason to kill him. Wasn't this just a robbery? They probably thought the office was empty because there were no cars in the driveway. Obviously, my father didn't need to drive since he could just walk back and forth."

"It's possible that's what happened. It's too early to say with certainty, but we have to look at all the angles."

"Oh, right. Of course."

"You said Dylan Johnson now handles the criminal cases. Has he had any concerns about his clients?"

"Not that he's mentioned."

"How did he get along with your father?"

Kyle was about to answer that they got along fine, when an idea flashed in his mind. He didn't have time to flesh it out now, but maybe it would be enough to plant a seed of doubt in the detective's mind and follow up later.

"They usually got along fine, but there seemed to be something off between them recently. I can't say what it was. More a feeling than anything else."

Detective Roberts's eyebrows lifted slightly and he made a notation in his notebook. Taking this as an opportunity, Kyle added, "I can look through my father's emails in case there was something in those, either with Dylan or someone else. It's possible my father hadn't mentioned it to anyone. He could be tightlipped." Even as he was speaking, the wheels in his head were turning. He already had the password to his father's email; another bit of subterfuge he'd accomplished in the past few months. It would take some time, but a few fake emails giving the impression of a rift between Caleb and Dylan could cast suspicion on Dylan and put him in the crosshairs of the investigation. "Would you be able to give me a few days to do that, though? I'll be needing to make arrangements for my father's funeral."

"Yes, of course. Here's my card," he said reaching into his pocket and handing one to Kyle. "If you would get back to me one way or the other if you've found anything, that would be very helpful. Assuming we haven't already caught the killer in the meantime."

Kyle took his wallet out of his suit jacket and inserted the card inside. *You can bet I will, and don't worry, Detective Roberts. You won't catch the killer before I get back to you,* he thought.

"Is there anything else I can help you with, Detective Roberts? I really do need to be making arrangements."

"You'll need to wait for the coroner to release his body before you can set an actual date, but I think I have all I need for today."

Kyle rose from his seat to accompany the detective out of the office.

"I do still need to interview Ms. Hayes or Ms. Foster. If you would show me where I can find my partner first?" Roberts reminded him.

"Oh, right. I'd forgotten. Follow me." Feeling confident now that he had a way to take the heat off himself, Kyle's mood lifted and a smile crossed his lips but he made sure to keep his demeanor polite. He was a grieving son, after all.

CHAPTER THREE: EVA

1

"Have you heard the news?"

Eva and Jim were sitting in their usual booth at The Checkout Diner, Glen Lake's only nod to a restaurant, when Betty Jones asked the question. She was the town's official gossip but most people overlooked that habit as she was never malicious. As the server at The Checkout, she was usually one of the first to hear any news about the town and its inhabitants.

"I don't think so. I've been busy sewing all morning and came straight here to meet Jim for lunch," Eva said.

"Me, either. I wasn't sewing all morning, but I haven't had the TV or radio on either," Jim smiled.

Betty's face lit up at the prospect of being the first to tell them.

"Caleb Mitchell was murdered last night. Amber found his body when she opened up the office this morning." Betty paused, waiting for the shock she expected to see on Jim and Eva's faces, and was not disappointed.

"Oh, my goodness! I was just there yesterday to sign my Will. What happened?" Eva asked.

"Are they sure it's murder?" Jim interjected before Betty had a chance to respond.

"The back door had been jimmied open and I was told it was a head wound, but that's not official. I got that secondhand from Frieda Nelson who heard it from Greg Landry. He's an EMT, you know?" She went on without waiting for an acknowledgement to the question. "And he was one of the first responders on the scene." She paused her narrative, waiting for their reactions to this bit of news.

Jim and Eva looked at each other, at a loss for what to say next.

"Who would want to kill Caleb?" Eva asked rhetorically.

"And why?" Jim asked.

"Maybe the evening news will have more about it," Betty offered.

"If you don't already know, my bet is that they don't either," Jim said, giving her a wink.

Betty beamed, taking his statement as a high compliment. "Now, are you ready to order the usual or do you need a minute to look at the menu?" she asked as she poured a mug of coffee for each of them.

"The usual," they answered in unison.

"It'll be ready in a jiffy!" Betty left to give their orders to Sam, the Diner's cook.

"I just don't know what to make of this," Eva said. "Why would anyone want to kill Caleb Mitchell?"

"He hasn't ever done any criminal defense work that I'm aware of so wouldn't have any disgruntled defendants who were sent to prison. I suppose it's possible he might have made a client unhappy, but angry enough to kill him? That doesn't seem plausible."

Eva nodded in agreement. "I think he did divorce work. It

might have been an angry ex-spouse of one of his clients. But to kill him?"

"That's a possibility. It might not have been the intention but things got out of hand."

"Or, it could have been one of those ex-spouses who can't handle losing their control. You know, the ones who ignore restraining orders and end up hurting or killing their exes. They might have gone after Caleb instead."

"Unfortunately, I do know. I only got involved in a couple situations like that during my career but even a couple is too many."

Jim was a retired state police officer.

Their discussion was interrupted by the arrival of their lunch orders.

"Thanks, Betty. I think this is a sign it's time to stop speculating about motives for murder and move on to other topics."

"Enjoy your meal!" Betty said and left to attend to her other diners.

"Speaking of which," Eva said. "How would you like to live with a cat?" She couldn't help but grin when Jim froze with his hands around his burger, held halfway between his plate and open mouth.

2

Is it that night again? Reuben was watching Eva as she cleaned the banquet tables set up in her sewing room.

"If you mean are the quilt club ladies coming, then, yes, it's that night again. And you mind your manners," she warned.

You wound me. I always mind my manners. Besides, unless you tell them what I've said, they have no idea if I've insulted them.

"That may be true, but your body language can speak volumes."

I'm a cat. It's my birthright to act the way I do.

"Nope. Not an excuse. They're my guests and I expect you to be courteous or if you can't, then find someplace else in the house where you can stay while they're here. Oh, that reminds me. Jim said he'd be happy to take you in if that becomes necessary."

Oh, happy days! I can hardly wait.

"You do remember that only happens if I die before you, right?"

It's a conundrum, isn't it? One of us is bound to lose in that scenario.

"Listen to you with your fifty cent words."

You sound as though you think I'm illiterate.

Eva noticed Reuben's tail was beginning to twitch and realized she'd gone too far.

"Just teasing, Reuben. I know you're smarter than the average bear."

We've been through this before. If that was supposed to be a compliment, I'm not impressed. I'm going to take a nap.

Eva chuckled beneath her breath as she watched him walk away and returned to her cleaning.

Her quilt club would be arriving that evening for their weekly meeting and potluck dinner. Potluck wasn't the best description since they each picked a slip of paper with a meal course written on it to ensure there would be a full course meal instead of four of the same dishes.

It may not be Reuben's favorite thing, but this club is one of the best things that's ever happened to me, she thought. *I can't imagine what my life would be like without Annalise, Jennifer, and Sarah in it. It would definitely be boring!*

The ladies met at Quilting Essentials, the local quilt shop, during a free motion quilting class. Once the class ended, they agreed to meet weekly at Eva's house. It was at their first meeting they discovered Eva wasn't the only one with special skills. Annalise Jordan was a psychic, Jennifer Ryder was able to do psychometry, and Sarah Pascal communicated with ghosts. Using those skills, they had solved four murders, creating an even stronger bond between them.

"That should do it," Eva said aloud as she surveyed her sewing studio. Shortly before retiring she had converted half of her two-car garage and turned it into the sewing studio of her dreams. Three folding banquet tables were ready for her guests to set up as their individual sewing stations. Her own sewing cabinet had a hydraulic lift for the machine to lower it to the same level as the cabinet top and a leaf that extended the surface area, making sewing large quilts a breeze. They shared the extra-large ironing board and cutting table. Bookcases were filled with fabric she bought over the years with the promise to herself that someday she would use it. *I should add something to my workbook about who to donate all of this to when I die,* she thought as she looked over her inventory. First choice would be given to the Club. *Might as well do that now while I'm thinking of it.*

Annalise and Jennifer are coming, Reuben announced to Eva later that afternoon.

She was so absorbed in a book, the sound of their cars pulling into the driveway hadn't penetrated into her consciousness. Sarah Pascal arrived just as she opened the door for the others, whose hands were full between their rolling sewing carts and dinner dishes.

"Why don't you take the food into the kitchen and I'll put it out while you set up your sewing stations," Eva suggested as the women filed in. Several minutes later they gathered in the dining room.

"I look forward to this every week almost as much as the sewing part," Sarah said. "It's so much fun to see what everybody has come up with."

"It's definitely another opportunity to be creative," Eva agreed. "I've even used that chicken recipe again for our strawberry theme."

Each week the ladies picked a theme for the potlucks and in

June, it had been strawberries to go with the local harvest time for the fruit. When she'd picked the slip for the entrée, she had thought it would be impossible, but finding a recipe using strawberries had been easier than Eva had imagined.

As the ladies sat down for their meal, the conversation turned to the news of Caleb Mitchell's murder.

"Betty Jones told Jim and me when we were at the Diner for lunch. I'd just been to his office the day before to sign my new Will," Eva told them.

"I learned about it when Kyle called us about what we'd need from him to put in an insurance claim," Jennifer said. She and her husband, David, owned the only insurance agency located in Glen Lake.

"How is he doing? He seemed distracted the day I was at the office," Eva said.

"He was all business but that may just be his way of holding himself together."

"I've seen them at some of the town events and I sensed they weren't close. If anything, Caleb treated Dylan more like his son. If I didn't know better, I would have thought Kyle was just one of the staff at the firm instead of the other way around," Annalise said.

"Caleb wasn't the warm and fuzzy type, but I can see how you'd think that. I'd thought it was because he and Dylan were lawyers and partners in the firm, so they had that bond in common. Now that you mention it, though, whenever I was in the office he did act more standoffish with Kyle," Eva said.

"Have they said anything on the news about a suspect?" Sarah asked.

"Not that I've heard. The back door had been broken into so it might have been a robbery. Even Betty didn't know, but that was a couple days ago. She may have the scoop by now even if the reporters don't," Eva said as everyone joined her laughter.

"Kyle hasn't given us an update yet but I think he might be

waiting for a copy of the police report to include with the claim if they find anything was stolen," Jennifer said.

"Jim and I were speculating about a motive. Other than computers, I wouldn't think there would be much to steal. We thought it could be a disgruntled client or ex of a client, but I'm sure we'll find out soon enough, either through the official news channels or Betty. Or maybe Annalise."

"Ha! I can't imagine why I would, but never say never. Messages sometimes come to me when I least expect them," Annalise replied.

"I had a thought earlier when I was looking over my fabric stash and thinking about my Will. Even after our crumb quilt project, I have a lot of scraps and the idea of doing a coin quilt came to me. It might be one of those stream of consciousness things. I went from having too much fabric to giving away my stuff when I die to money and then coin quilts. Please tell me it's not just me who thinks like that," Eva said, blushing.

"I resemble that remark," Jennifer reassured her.

"I'm still new to this. What's a coin quilt?" Sarah asked.

"It's a strip quilt, or can be. You can make them whatever width you want, but it's rows of the strips and can have a solid sashing in between them. Here, let me show you. I was looking it up while Eva was talking," Annalise said, handing over her phone for Sarah to inspect.

"Oh, that would be perfect for using up the leftover strips from the jelly roll I bought to do the Halloween banner. It has my vote!" Sarah said, handing Annalise's phone back to her.

"I'm in," Jennifer said.

"Me, too. I've been promising myself to use up more of my scrap stash so no need for more excuses with this pattern," Annalise agreed.

"It's unanimous! How about we take the rest of the meeting to find which one we want to make and what size? I'll bring out my laptop and you can go through my quilt books. There must be at least one coin quilt among the dozens of books I have," Eva offered. "Or go straight to your machine if you've brought a project to work on and want to pick a pattern later. We can concentrate on quilts tonight instead of finding a killer."

"I'm all in favor of that, too!" Annalise said, and the others nodded in agreement.

An hour later the meeting adjourned on a high note, everyone excited at the prospect of beginning a new quilt project that would use up their scraps. For once, solving a crime hadn't been part of the program.

3

"Hi, Jennifer. I'm calling to see if you would like to go with me today to sign up for the longarm quilting class at Quilting Essentials?"

"I'd love to! I have today off so it's perfect timing. Do you think Annalise might like to come with us?" Jennifer asked.

"I'll give her a call. She might have clients today. I should probably text Sarah to ask if she'd like us to sign her up, too. I hate to bother her while she's working but a text is usually okay. Why don't we meet at the shop in half an hour either way? If Annalise can't go, we can sign up for her."

"Sounds like a plan. See you soon!"

"Annalise, it's Eva. Are you busy today? Jennifer and I are going to Quilting Essentials to sign up for the longarm class that she told us about a couple months ago."

"That sounds like fun. I have a client later this afternoon but I can go this morning," Annalise said.

"Perfect! We're meeting there in half an hour."

Eva texted Sarah and was surprised to immediately receive a reply.

Thanks for the invite! Can't come today but
please do sign me up for the class. I'll make it
work whenever it's available.

Eva replied with a thumbs up emoji.

"I'm going out for a while, Reuben. Hold down the fort while I'm gone."

I heard. Yes, I was eavesdropping. Take your time. I could use some alone time to catch up on my beauty sleep.

"You're purrrfect just as you are, Reuben, but enjoy your nap!" she said pronouncing the word so that Reuben understood what she was doing.

Oh, brother. I can't believe you said that! Reuben turned and stalked off to his favorite cushion in the bay window.

Eva arrived at Quilting Essentials a short time later. It was located in a strip mall not far from her house and didn't require driving all the way into Bangor, which she considered a plus. *Now, remember, you're only here to sign up for the class. You do not need any more fabric!* she reminded herself. The angel on her other shoulder was tempted by the display of holiday fabrics which had been added since the last time she was in the store. The owner, Evelyn Jackson, looked up from the shelf she was stocking with pre-cuts at the sound of the bell chiming when Eva opened the door.

"Hello, Eva, can I help you with something or are you just browsing?"

"My reason for coming was to sign up for the longarm quilting class. Jennifer and Annalise will be coming soon, too. I swear I'm just like one of Pavlov's dogs. I'm not salivating like they did, but as soon as I see all this fabric and kits for different projects, my head starts spinning thinking about all the things I could make.. someday. I promised myself I would not buy any fabric today, though. We'll see if I can stick to it."

Evelyn chuckled. "I hear that a lot. Luckily for me, not everyone can resist."

The sound of the chime made them turn toward the door and they were greeted by Jennifer and Annalise.

"Eva told me you're here to sign up for the longarm class. I'll go get my class schedule and be right back."

"These holiday prints are so pretty," Jennifer said as she examined the bolts of cloth.

"I thought the same thing when I spied them. I *want* them but I do not *need* them. Be sure to tell me that if I look as though I'm going to take them to the cutting counter."

"Only if you do the same for me," Annalise said.

Evelyn returned, holding a wire-bound calendar planner. "Okay, it looks like I'll have slots for the classes in two weeks. I usually only do two people at a time. Did all three of you want to take the class?"

"We do, but Sarah Pascal would like to take it, too. She wasn't able to come in person but she asked me to sign her up and it didn't matter what day or time."

"Wonderful! Who wants to go first?"

"I can't do any on Thursdays. I'm at the office with David," Jennifer said.

Annalise pulled out her phone and scrolled to her calendar. "I can do that Thursday since it's in the afternoon. I only have two clients in the morning." Annalise was a Reiki practitioner who worked from home, giving her the ability to set her own schedule.

"I can do that Thursday but if Sarah finds out she can't take the Wednesday class after all, I can switch with her," Eva said. "I can't wait! The coin quilt will be a great project to do an allover pattern and on a longarm, it would take no time at all."

"Learning how to use a pantograph is part of the lesson," Evelyn said.

Jennifer's eyebrows knit together. "What's a pantograph?"

"They're quilt designs on a long piece of paper that we put on the back side of the longarm machine. As you trace the design, the machine stitches the pattern onto the quilt. They're perfect for doing an allover design on larger quilts. We have several different patterns, but you can find more online. If you see one you want to order, bring it with you to the class and you can practice using it."

"Now I'm even more excited to take the class," Eva face lit up. "I'm so glad you told us about this, Jennifer."

"Me, too!" Annalise added. "I've got all kinds of projects going through my head that I want to try once I learn how to do this."

"I'll pencil you in for those days and it doesn't matter to me which class you show up for as long as I have it in my scheduler that the two slots are filled. Otherwise, I'll put someone else in for that class." She finished writing in their names and then a sad expression crossed her face. "That was horrible news about Caleb Mitchell." Evelyn was another resident of Glen Lake, along with Eva, Annalise, and Jennifer.

"Has there been any news about whether they decided if it was a robbery gone wrong or a disgruntled client?" Annalise asked.

"I don't think so. From what I've been told, they're still trying to figure that out. There haven't been any other robberies in town recently that I'm aware of but that doesn't mean it wasn't one," Evelyn said.

"It's only been a few days. They're probably doing interviews and gathering evidence. I might ask Jim if he's heard anything. He still has friends on the police force who might have information that's okay to pass along," Eva said. She looked around the shop with a wistful expression.

"I see that look on your face," Annalise said. "Can you be trusted to just look around or is it time for us to go?" she teased.

"Maybe just one walk around the shop in case I find something besides material that I can't live without or forgot I needed. You know, while I'm here anyway," Eva said, returning Annalise's smile.

"We should make a pact. If anyone needs to be told to use their willpower, speak up," Jennifer suggested.

They each put one hand out as the others stacked theirs on top. "Deal!"

CHAPTER FOUR: KYLE

1

The excuse Kyle had given Detective Roberts about needing more time to plan Caleb's funeral had been a half-truth. His father had been a compulsively organized person and that included making plans for his funeral, right down to the music that should be played during the service and the passages he wanted to have read. Kyle was surprised he hadn't written his own eulogy. For once Caleb's control issues worked to Kyle's advantage, giving him more time to put his plan into place to frame Dylan. He was going to have to push Dylan to hire another lawyer sooner than later. If Dylan went to jail, the firm would have to close if they didn't already have someone to take his place, and that would mean he'd be out of a job. Caleb had been well-to-do, but Kyle's inheritance wouldn't be enough to retire early, especially not the way Erica spent money. It would at least get him out of his current financial difficulties so he could breathe a little easier, and there might even be some left over to put into the college funds for the kids. Erica couldn't touch that. He'd made sure of it.

The office was still off-limits so he was working at home and Erica was out shopping. As she'd put it, she couldn't possibly wear any of the black outfits already in her closet for Caleb's funeral and the kids would need new outfits, too. He hadn't bothered arguing when she'd come up with her justification for the new clothes being, what would people think if they weren't presentable? *Any excuse to go shopping, right, Erica?* After notifying the funeral home and church that their time would be needed as soon as the coroner released Caleb's body and a call to the Ryder Insurance Agency about his life insurance policy, he began drafting the fake emails between Caleb and Dylan. He'd had some help from an AI site giving it the prompt of *Please write a series of emails between an employer and employee in which the employee is upset with his employer and becomes threatening over time. This will be used as part of the plot of a murder mystery novel in which the employee ends up killing his employer.* It had taken only seconds for the AI to come back with a reply. After a few tweaks, Kyle had something he could work with. He'd need to phrase them more in Caleb and Dylan's style and voice but it was a good start and saved him hours of time. With the password to Caleb's computer, he could easily send emails to Dylan that would look genuine once he'd manipulated the metadata. More of a challenge would be faking the emails Dylan "sent" to Caleb. Kyle tapped his pen on his desk as he deliberated how to access the password for Dylan's computer.

An idea began to form in his mind. There are burner phones but what about a burner tablet? That would eliminate the password problem altogether. He would buy a tablet and set it up in Dylan's name and use some of the information he already had in his personnel file, along with a new email account. If he used cash to buy the device, he wouldn't leave a paper trail. He would have to drive out of town to make sure no one local saw him purchase it, but Ellsworth or Waterville were close enough to drive there and back within a few hours. He'd have to find a place to stash it in the office that would make it appear like Dylan had hidden it but then the detectives would have to find it somehow. The plan wasn't perfect, but Kyle thought it was a good start. Once he got everything set up, he would "find" the messages on Caleb's computer and then tell Roberts about them to start the ball rolling.

Kyle began humming softly as he opened a new browser window in Incognito mode, and searched for tablets online, beginning in Ellsworth since it was closer, and his spirits began to lift.

2

The church was packed for the funeral. It seemed that everyone in town had turned out for it. Kyle sat in the front pew with Erica and the kids and kept his eyes forward. Erica had organized a reception in the church basement following the graveside service and he'd be expected to interact then. He'd made it through the two days of visitor hours at the funeral home, his muscles tightening as he held in what he wanted to say whenever someone told him what a kind and generous man Caleb had been. *Yes, he had a stern outer appearance but underneath that he'd had a heart of gold and contributed so much to the community. He would be missed.* They wouldn't be saying that if he'd been their father. *Why was it he could be like that to everyone else, but when it came to him... his own family... he wouldn't lend a hand and treated him like he was a leech if he asked for help?*

Thankfully, all of those who'd been at the church didn't come to the reception. Erica was mingling with the crowd, in her element as hostess despite the reason for the gathering. Kyle had to admit she'd outdone herself with the reception. The catered food was topnotch and everyone seemed to be enjoying it, if the speed at which it was disappearing was any judge. Kyle was standing by himself off to the side in the back of the room, sipping punch from a plastic cup when he spotted Detectives Smith and Roberts near the entrance at the front of the room. He tossed the now empty cup in the bin marked for Recyclables and walked toward them.

"Detectives, thank you for coming," he said, shaking their hands. The line had become rote after having repeated it so many times over the past few days, but Kyle aimed for sincerity even more than usual. He wanted to keep the illusion of grieving, but dignified, son intact especially for them. When it came time to frame Dylan, he wanted to be past any hint of suspicion as a suspect.

"Again, we're sorry for your loss," Detective Roberts was the first to respond.

"Your father must have been very well-regarded in the community judging by the number of mourners who showed up at the services and now here," Detective Smith commented.

"Yes." Kyle nodded his head in agreement. "He'd lived in Glen Lake for more than forty years and between the law practice and volunteering in the community, there probably wasn't anyone in town who didn't know him." Kyle paused for what he thought was an appropriate amount of time before getting to the real reason he'd come to speak to them. "Have you had any leads in the investigation of his murder?"

"No, not yet. The only prints we were able to identify belonged to everyone who worked at the office. There were others, but none were in the system so unless we're able to eliminate them as clients, we'll have to keep them on file for when we get a break in the case. Client confidentiality is a roadblock with asking for names for the elimination process."

Detective Roberts picked up the narrative. "We've questioned his neighbors, but no one saw anything unusual that night. Have you had the opportunity to go through the client files for any who might have been dissatisfied with the firm's services, in particular your father's?"

"No, I'm sorry. I've been preoccupied with the funeral, but now that that's done and we've been given the okay to open the office, I'll make that our priority."

"Thank you. It will be a big help. I think that should do it for now. We'll let you go back to your guests," Detective Roberts said.

Kyle shook their hands and watched through the window as they walked to their cars and went on their way. The sound of laughter behind him caught his attention. His eyes narrowed and his chest tightened as he located its source. A small group was clustered around Dylan. The ease with which Dylan so easily interacted with others grated on Kyle, reminding him of his own social awkwardness. *He won't be laughing for long*, Kyle promised himself and walked toward the group.

3

Kyle sat at the head of the conference room table facing Dylan at the opposite end and Amber and Grace sat on either side. He'd emailed everyone the night before that he wanted a staff meeting before they officially opened the office. He sat straighter than usual and had a sense of confidence now that he was in charge; something he'd never felt when his father was alive.

"Detectives Roberts and Smith asked me if we know of any past or current clients who might have had a grudge against my father. Amber, have you seen any correspondence or taken any phone calls recently that are in that category?"

"I can't think of any recently, but there have been some in the past. I'll need to go through the files and client list to refresh my memory. It shouldn't be busy this morning since we rescheduled clients to begin coming back tomorrow. I'll make that my first priority."

"Thank you. Dylan, we'll need to hire another attorney to fill Dad's place as soon as possible. Do you have anyone in mind who might be a good candidate?"

"I have a couple ideas. I'm sure between myself and Grace we can keep things running long enough to take our time finding the right person, though. It might mean some extra hours for me, but I don't mind. I'd much rather get it right than hire someone who isn't a good fit for everyone. Why the rush?"

Kyle looked down at the open folder in front of him as a flash of anger came over him. His jaw clenched and he drew his lips together in a thin line. *Be cool. No arguments.* He slowly took a deep breath in and out through his nose and consciously relaxed his jaw and mouth before meeting Dylan's eyes and responding.

"You're absolutely right. We want to make sure whoever we hire is the right person for the job but we don't have any idea how long it might take. We should at least begin looking. I wouldn't want to overburden you and Grace or give our clients less than the best service possible." He forced himself to give Dylan an *I'm just looking out for you, buddy* smile.

Dylan looked back at him a little longer than Kyle felt was necessary, but then nodded.

"Of course. I'll put out some feelers this morning."

"Amber, have you had a chance to make a list of all the client cases my father was working on so Dylan and Grace can decide who should take responsibility for them in the meantime?"

"Yes, but I thought they might want to see the actual case files and I haven't been able to pull any of them yet. I was going to do that this morning."

"Do you need any help with that? Maybe Grace can give you a hand." He looked at Grace for her response.

"Sure, I can help. I have some work to do but it isn't urgent."

She turned to Dylan. "Is there a good time this afternoon that we can get together?"

Kyle sat back with his elbows resting on the arms of the chair and his hands steepled under his chin. This was going just as planned. He would wait at least a few days before informing the detectives about the emails he'd found between "Dylan" and Caleb. He already knew about the other cases that Amber would find, or at least the ones his father had told him about. It would give her something to do and might even work to his advantage. Giving the detectives those names and circumstances would be a good distraction while they investigated those leads. Pointing the finger at Dylan so soon might be too obvious, he reasoned. Yes, it was all coming together. He could be patient. After all, didn't they always say good things come to those who wait? The hint of a smile crossed his lips as he imagined the outcome of his planning coming to fruition. *You always thought you were so smart. Who's the smart one now, Dylan?*

4

"Detective Smith, this is Kyle Mitchell. Have you had a chance to follow up on the list of names we sent over?"

"We have, Mr. Mitchell, but they all had solid alibis for the time of the murder."

"I may have new information for you. I've gone through my father's personal computer and found an encrypted file but I was able to locate the password in my father's safe in his home office. The file contained PDF copies of some disturbing emails my father had received. He had exported them from his email account which is why I hadn't seen them when I went through his emails." He paused to let that sink in with the detective.

"Who were the emails from?"

"You may remember I'd mentioned at our first meeting that I

thought something was off between my father and Dylan Johnson. The emails were between them. I had no idea the extent of
the animosity he held against my father, but the emails show a
very different picture of what was going on behind the scenes."

"Can you elaborate?"

"Dylan was insisting on receiving a larger share of the part-
nership. He claimed he was carrying the bulk of the firm's case
load and should receive at least twenty percent more than he is
currently being paid. My father refused and that's when things
turned ugly. Dylan threatened to do a hostile takeover and force
my father out if he didn't get what he wanted."

"Would you forward those communications to me? Detective
Roberts and I will look them over and follow up with you."

"Of course, I'm happy to do that. I hope I'm making more of
this than there is. It seems so out of character for Dylan but
sometimes people aren't who you think they are on the surface."

Kyle disconnected the call and forwarded the file. Phase One
accomplished. This weekend he would come into the office and
plant the tablet with Dylan's side of the emails. He'd wait until
Monday to let the detectives know he'd found it. He couldn't
wait to see the look on Dylan's face when they came in with a
search warrant and took him out in handcuffs.

5

Kyle told Erica he was going out for doughnuts as a treat for
the kids on Sunday morning but first he was going to the office
to hide the tablet. He breathed a sigh of relief when no one was
parked in the driveway when he arrived. He wasn't the only one
with a key and it wouldn't be out of character for Dylan to come
in if he needed a file. They'd both been in on a Sunday morning
in the past, but so far, luck was with him today. He picked up the
tablet which he'd wiped down with alcohol before placing it in a

plastic bag. He'd brought gloves to put on before taking it out. Not having any fingerprints, especially Dylan's, on it might be a problem but it was possible the detectives would think he'd wiped them off himself so he could claim it wasn't his. After all, he was a lawyer and knew he could defend himself if he tried to say it wasn't his because there weren't prints on it.

But what about the emails on Caleb's computer? How are you going to explain that, Dylan?

He went into Dylan's office and looked around for a likely hiding spot. It would need to be tucked away so he wouldn't find it before the detectives had a chance to get there. Not in his desk. Much too easy for him to find it there.

Where would I hide you if I was Dylan?

If you were Dylan, you wouldn't be doing this in the first place.

The rejoinder caught him by surprise and a twinge of guilt overcame him, but only for a moment. It was only in his head but it felt like something Caleb would have said to him.

If you'd loaned me the money, I wouldn't have *to be doing this.*

That thought set his resolve. It was too late now, anyway. He'd already set the deeds in motion when he told the detectives about the emails. They'd be following up so he had to continue with his plan and it was crucial for them to find the tablet. His eyes landed on the credenza. He'd never looked inside it before so didn't know what he would find. He opened the first drawer and found hanging folders with client intake folders. There were digital files, of course, but Caleb insisted everyone keep hard copies as well. No amount of argument that the digital files were backed up on a secure cloud server had dissuaded him, so it was easier to do as he asked. Kyle closed the drawer and went on to the next one and found a stack of blank legal pads and empty file folders. This had potential. He debated between putting it in one of the folders or underneath the legal pads. He laid the tablet down on top of the credenza and put on the gloves he'd stuck in his jacket pocket. He removed the tablet from the plastic bag and held it a moment longer as he looked from the pads to the files and ultimately, decided to tuck it underneath the pads. There were enough there that it was unlikely Dylan would find it. It was only logical that he'd take a pad from the top of the pile if he needed one. Satisfied with his choice, Kyle closed the drawer and picked up the bag he'd brought it in and went back to his car, making sure to lock the door behind him.

The corners of his mouth turned up in a slight smile as he hummed along with the radio and drove into Bangor for the doughnuts he'd promised to bring home.

CHAPTER FIVE: DYLAN

1

I t was after hours, but Dylan wanted to finish prepping for his first appointment with a new client the next day before going home for the evening. He opened the case file to read through the questionnaire the client had completed and flipped the page on his legal pad to take notes, only to find he'd used the last blank page. He wasn't paying attention so hadn't realized it had been mixed into the rest of the now completely filled pad. He exhaled audibly with annoyance and tossed his pen on his desk. He took a new one from the credenza but as he was closing the drawer in which they were stored, the pads shifted and a glint of silver appeared underneath them, catching his attention. *What the heck?* Moving the pads aside, he discovered a tablet that wasn't his. Curious now, he pushed the power button on and the device came to life. The home screen appeared without requiring a password or security code and displayed the usual apps pre-loaded on this type of tablet, but the one for mail drew his eye. His nerves tingled with a sense of foreboding as he tapped the icon. Once again, the app opened without a need for a password and a list of emails filled the screen. He recognized Caleb's email address but not the address for the person on the other end of the conversations. He opened the most recent one and caught his breath when he read the message. The signature at the end of the email was his. Scrolling to the bottom of the list to begin with the oldest email, he opened the communications one by one, stunned by what he was reading. They started out civilly, but by the last email had taken on a threatening tone toward Caleb. His stomach knotted as he realized he was being set up because all the email threats were signed *Dylan,* clearly implicating him. There was no other explanation for why the tablet had been hidden in his office. He knew exactly how this would look if the police had found it first. The only possibility was it had been put in his credenza by someone in the office and he suspected who that someone was. It had to be Kyle. *But why?*

2

Dylan slipped the tablet into his briefcase. He considered wiping it to remove his fingerprints but changed his mind. It wasn't likely, but in the off-chance Kyle had been careless, his prints might be on it and he didn't want to wipe those off inadvertently. His mind swirled during the drive home. He was aware that Kyle had always been jealous of him, but would he really go to these lengths to frame him for Caleb's murder? Did Kyle really expect the police who were investigating the case to think he had killed Caleb when they found the tablet? The only reason someone tries to deflect attention onto someone else is when they're the one who is guilty. *It was obvious they didn't have a close relationship but would Kyle really have gone to the extreme of killing him? And why?* He didn't want to believe Kyle would be capable of it, but still…

Love and money. Those are the usual motives for people killing each other, Dylan thought. *Love doesn't seem like the likely reason, so it must be money.* Dylan thought about Kyle's fancy house and from what he'd seen of Erica, shopping could be her middle name. And it was only the high-end label items that would do. He hadn't checked the financial reports recently to see how much Kyle was paid, but it would take a lot to keep up with those expenses. The more he thought about the possibilities, the more convinced he became that it was Kyle. There was no way a random burglar would have concocted such an elaborate plan and it was a lot to think even a disgruntled client would do it.

Okay, but now what do you do about it? The logical thing would be to call the homicide detectives and report finding the tablet. If he was guilty of being the one who'd sent those emails, it wouldn't make sense that he would be the one reporting it to the police, so he wasn't worried about that. *What if you use it as a way to trap Kyle if that's his next play?* That thought tipped the scales. He'd like to have more information about them first, though.

By that time, he'd reached his house and was pulling into the driveway, Christopher Davis was parking in his driveway next door. Dylan remembered Christopher's dad, Jim, was a retired cop. He'd been a state trooper but he might have had interactions with the detectives over the years or know someone else who had.

"Christopher, do you have a minute?" Dylan called out through his opened passenger window. He'd caught him just as Christopher was about to open his front door but looked over when he heard his name.

"Sure, what can I do for you?"

"I was hoping you could put me in touch with your dad. I'd like to ask him if he knows the detectives investigating Caleb's murder."

Christopher smiled before replying, "You're in luck. Dad's coming over for dinner tonight. He should be here any minute now. Do you need to talk to him right away or can this wait until after we've eaten?"

"It's not urgent. Give me a call when you're ready."

Dylan powered the window back up and pulled into his garage. The entrance from the garage opened into a mudroom and then into the spacious kitchen. The aroma of spaghetti sauce filled his nostrils and his stomach growled, reminding him of how long it had been since breakfast when he'd last eaten.

"That smells delicious," he said, leaning down to give his wife, Natalie, a peck on the cheek. "How long until dinner's ready?"

"Not long. The lasagna needs to rest and I have garlic bread warming up in the oven. You've got time to change into your jeans and a tee. While you're upstairs, would you tell Ryan and Alex they've got fifteen minutes before dinner? They're supposed to be doing their homework, but we're dealing with teenagers, so it wouldn't surprise me if you found them playing their video games."

"Can do. How was your day?"

"A bad car accident, a sprained ankle from a football injury, a case of appendicitis. You know, the usual boring day," Natalie replied, tongue in cheek. In her job as an RN in the ER of Bangor Medical Center, she rarely had a boring day. "How about you?"

Dylan hesitated about whether to mention the tablet. "I'll tell you later. Right now, I should go change and get the kids. I have something to do after dinner with Christopher and his dad. I'll explain everything after I've had a chance to talk to them."

Natalie tilted her head and frowned. "Sounds mysterious."

"Could be. I promise I'll fill you in on all the deets later."

He gave her another kiss before leaving to change. On his way to his own bedroom, he knocked on Ryan's door and then Alex's. "Mom says dinner's ready in fifteen." He heard a muffled okay from each of them and continued walking to his room.

3

As soon as Jim walked into the living room, he was greeted enthusiastically by his seventeen-year-old granddaughter, Danielle, and fifteen-year-old grandson, Gavin.

"I didn't think anything would get them to pause a video game, but you managed it," Christopher said with amazement.

"That's the power of grandparents," Jim said, winking. "What are you kids playing?" he asked, turning his attention to the teenagers.

"Zelda," Gavin replied. "It's been out a while but we still have levels we didn't get to before."

"And I'm winning," Danielle gloated.

Gavin gave her a scathing glance. "You cheated."

"No, I didn't. You're just a sore loser."

"On that note, I'm going to go say hello to Olivia. Is she in the kitchen?" Jim asked.

"She's finishing up dinner," Christopher replied. "Which reminds me, you two need to get the table set. Dinner will be ready soon."

They started to object but the warning look Jim gave them stopped them cold. They turned off the video game and went to the kitchen for plates and utensils.

"Also, the power of grandparents," Jim told Christopher. Christopher just shook his head choosing not to argue his father's logic.

"Olivia, is that my favorite roast chicken recipe I'm smelling?" Jim asked, giving her a kiss on the cheek.

"It is. With all the trimmings just like you like them," his daughter-in-law replied with a smile. "It will be ready in about five minutes. I just need to mash the potatoes."

"So, tell me about how it's going in school this year," Jim asked once they were all seated at the table.

"I made the basketball varsity team," Gavin said, his chest puffed out with pride.

"Congratulations! Make sure you get me the game schedule so I can come watch you play."

"I'll make a copy for you after dinner," Olivia said.

"How about you, Danielle? Have you started your college applications?"

"I'm applying to UMaine. That's my first choice, but I'm going to put in applications to Northeastern and the University of New England in Biddeford."

"She wants to go to UMaine to be with her *boy* friend," Gavin said with a smug expression.

Danielle glared at her brother.

"Gavin, be nice," Christopher warned.

"Yes, Dad," he said, and concentrated on his dinner.

"You've got a boyfriend? Who is he? Should I have my police buddies do a background check?" Jim said, giving Christopher a wink.

"Grampa!" Danielle objected. "You know him, don't you? It's Matt Ryder, Jennifer's son."

Jim's eyebrows raised. "You don't say. Well, in that case, you picked a good one."

"Oh, I almost forgot! When I was coming home, Dylan asked me if you'd be willing to talk to him tonight. He wanted to know if you could tell him what you think about the detectives handling Caleb Mitchell's murder."

"Really?" Jim raised his eyebrows. "Sure, I'd be happy to. Is he having a problem with them?"

"He didn't say and I didn't ask. I figured we'd find out when you talked to him. *If* you did," he added realizing he'd made an assumption about Jim's willingness. "I told him I'd let him know after dinner."

"Do you know who they are?"

"No. Another question I thought could wait. Sorry."

"No worries. I might not know them, but I'm happy to help if I can." Jim turned his attention to Olivia. "What's new in your world, Liv?"

"Same stuff, different day. Take money in, give money out. I can barely keep it together with all the excitement," she said, smiling. "Seriously, though, being a bank teller might not be the most riveting job, but I'm grateful to have the paycheck with tuition for two kids going to college coming up ahead of us."

"Don't forget I've put money into a college fund for them. It might only be enough to pay for books these days, but I hope it will help."

"Thanks, Dad. It's appreciated. We should probably finish up," Christopher said, looking at his watch.

"Are you coming right back?" Gavin asked.

"It shouldn't take too long. In the meantime, you can pass the time by helping your mother clean up and get your homework done," Christopher said.

"And Zelda stays off until it is," Olivia said, giving both teenagers a pointed look.

"Yes, Mom," they answered together in a sing-song tone.

"If you're all set, Dad, I'll give Dylan a call to say we're coming over."

"Yup. Thanks for dinner, Olivia, It was delicious, as always."

"Dylan's ready for us," Christopher said after disconnecting the call.

"Okay, let's make like a tree and leaf," Jim said, and was rewarded with groans from both teenagers.

4

"Thanks for dinner! That was even more delicious than it smelled, Nat," Dylan said.

Ryan, the eighteen-year-old, let out a loud belch. "My compliments to the chef," he said, eliciting a side-eye from Natalie and an eye-roll from fifteen-year-old Alex.

Dylan and Natalie shook their heads and exchanged parental

glances that conveyed their resignation of expecting more from Ryan's table manners. Natalie shrugged her shoulders as if to say, "at least he doesn't do that in public."

"A simple 'that was really good, Mom,' would also do, but thank you."

Dylan wiped his mouth and laid his napkin beside his plate before pushing back his chair and standing. "You two help your Mom clean up. I'm going up to my office to wait for Christopher to call. I'm not sure if he and Jim are coming here or I'll be going to Christopher's house," he said. Thinking of Natalie's earlier comment, he added, "And make sure your homework is done before any more video games."

"All done, Dad. Had it finished before dinner," Alex said.

"Me, too," Ryan said, picking up his plate and stacking Dylan's on top of it.

"I'm not sure how long I'll be, but I'm hoping I'll be done before you go to bed," he told Natalie. She worked the morning shift at the hospital so was early-to-bed and early-to-rise.

"I hope so, too. You have my curiosity piqued."

Dylan gave her a smile and a wink and went to his office to await Christopher and Jim's arrival.

Fifteen minutes later Dylan's phone rang and Christopher's name appeared on the screen.

"Hi, Christopher. Thanks for calling. Should I come to your house or could your dad come to mine?"

"We can come to you. The kids need to finish their homework and Grampa can be a distraction," Christopher said with a chuckle.

"I get that! Meet me at my office in the garage. I'll leave the garage door unlocked."

Two minutes later he heard the sound of a knock on his door and then Christopher's voice calling out, "Dylan, it's Chris and Jim."

"Come on upstairs," Dylan called back and walked over to the stairway to greet them. "Good to see you again, Jim.

Thanks for coming," he said as he led them into his home office.

"Always glad to help a neighbor out," Jim replied. "Christopher told me you asked him if I'm familiar with the detectives assigned to Caleb's case."

"That's right. Their names are Phil Rogers and Dennis Smith."

"Oh, yes, I do know them. They're standup guys and they'll do their best to solve the case."

"Good to know. Do you think they are the type who follow up on all leads and can keep an open mind? Say, even if they are given evidence that might incriminate someone who's innocent?"

Jim looked Dylan straight in the eye and Dylan could tell he was calculating why he was asking the question.

"My experience with them is that they would. Am I correct in suspecting this is more than just a hypothetical question?"

Dylan hesitated. He wasn't well-acquainted with Jim, but from the few times they had socialized, he knew he could trust him. He opened the briefcase which he'd placed on top of his desk and pulled out the tablet.

"I found this under a stack of legal pads in my credenza this afternoon. It's not mine and I don't know for sure where it came from but I think Kyle Mitchell may be trying to frame me for Caleb's murder."

Christopher's shocked expression was in sharp contrast to Jim's neutral countenance. His eyebrows had lifted slightly but otherwise showed no surprise. Dylan attributed that to Jim's years as a trooper.

"What makes you think that?" Jim asked.

"I was able to access the email app and found a chain of communications between Caleb and someone named Dylan. It wasn't me but I'm convinced the intent is to make the police think it is. They start out innocently enough, but the tone changes and by the end, *Dylan*," he said using air quotes, "was threatening Caleb. I recognize Caleb's email address as the one he used but I've never had an email address like the one in these emails."

Jim nodded but was quiet. Dylan waited patiently for him to reply.

"I'm guessing you want to turn in the tablet but you want to make sure the detectives will hear you out. We both know you don't have a choice about that because you don't want to be guilty of withholding evidence. Before you do, though, I have another idea. This is where I ask if you have an open mind because what I'm about to suggest is going to require you to suspend your disbelief. Have you heard of psychometry?"

5

"I've heard the word, but I don't remember its meaning," Dylan said, his brows furrowed in confusion.

"I know someone who has that gift. She's used it to help solve four murders. If you can give me a minute, I'll give her a call now, but I don't want to say more without her permission. It's not something she makes a habit of letting become public knowledge and I want to respect her confidentiality."

"What does that have to do with the tablet?" Christopher asked.

"Sometimes when she holds an object, she gets impressions about it. She might be able to discover information about who planted it in Dylan's office."

A look of understanding came over both Christopher and Dylan's faces.

"I'll be right back. I'll go outside to make the call."

"No need, Jim. Christopher and I can go downstairs while you make the call. It's a little too cold tonight to be standing outside having a phone conversation."

Once they were out of earshot, Jim scrolled to his Contacts for Jennifer Ryder's number. They had first become acquainted when Jennifer's great-aunt Sadie had been murdered and Jim accompanied her to the police to give them evidence about the identity of the killer. Luck was with him when she answered the call instead of going to voicemail.

"Jim, what a nice surprise!"

"I hope you'll still think so when I tell you why." Jim didn't want to influence her so explained that Dylan could use her help with a legal situation involving a tablet. "Would you be willing to come to Dylan's house and use your psychometry to pick up impressions about the owner of the tablet?"

There was silence on the line and Jim knew Jennifer was considering his request and the ramifications if she accepted. He gave her time to think it over, and at last she replied.

"I'm happy to help. I think I can trust Dylan to not tell anyone else about my gift."

"Would you mind if my son, Christopher, is here, too?"

Jennifer hesitated for only a second. "If he's at all like you, I have no doubt I can trust him, too."

Jennifer arrived at Dylan's house thirty minutes later. After introductions were made, Dylan brought out the tablet and held it out for her inspection.

"Before I take it, I want to explain about the way this works for me. I'll hold the object and if I make a connection, images will appear in my mind. It doesn't always happen, but I'll do what I can. Did Jim mention to you that I'd like to keep this between us? It's a small town and I don't want to put David's insurance agency at risk of people thinking he's got a weirdo working there. If he wanted to marry one, that's one thing, but they might think differently about their willingness to do business with us." Her lips curved in a smile as she finished but they all understood she was determined about keeping her ability a secret.

"Of course," Dylan replied. "I live and work here, too, so I completely understand how that would affect you and David."

"Your secret's safe with me, too," Christopher said.

"When you mentioned this was connected to a legal situation, Jim, it occurred to me that it would be best if my fingerprints weren't on the tablet so I brought a pair of gloves just in case. She removed them from her purse. Will I need these?"

Jim caught himself just in time. He was about to tease her about being a psychic like Annalise, forgetting for a moment that Dylan and Christopher didn't know about that.

"Good thinking, Jen. Yes, that's a great idea."

"Okay, let me see what comes up," Jennifer said, taking the tablet from Dylan after putting on the gloves. She closed her eyes and held it with both hands in her lap as three pairs of eyes watched and waited. Her breathing slowed and her eyelids began almost imperceptibly moving, like someone dreaming. After a few minutes she opened her eyes and let out a deep breath through her mouth.

"Wow, I can't believe what came to me, but it's so far-fetched that I can't imagine it couldn't be true. Kyle Mitchell is the one who bought this and is responsible for the emails on it. He's trying to set you up, Dylan. He's trying to put the blame on you for killing Caleb, but he's the one who did it."

6

The three men exchanged glances, although Jim's didn't register the surprise that Dylan's and Christopher's did. He'd been a witness to this before. Dylan leaned forward in his chair with his hands clasped on his knees.

"Can you describe for me exactly what you saw?" he asked Jennifer, an intense expression on his face.

"Would you like me to wait while you find a legal pad?" she asked, but the smile on her face let him know she was teasing.

"I'm sorry, what?" he asked, his brows furrowed in confusion and then it dawned on him what she meant and he smiled sheepishly. "I guess that did come out more in lawyer mode than I intended. Occupational hazard."

"It's okay. I knew where it was coming from. The first impression I got was Kyle buying the tablet. He paid cash and I didn't recognize the store he was in so I'm guessing he went out of town for it. The next image was him in Caleb's office. I recognized it from the times David and I have been there to have legal work done. He was at the desktop computer and had the tablet on the desk, too. I saw him type an email on Caleb's computer, waited for it to ping on the tablet, and then typed a message on that. I had the sense he continued on like that for some time even though he had a handwritten page that it looked like he was copying. It was as though he'd prepared the emails ahead of time and was transcribing them. When he was done, he took the tablet into another office and went to the credenza. He opened one of the drawers and put the tablet underneath a stack of legal pads. I'm guessing that office must have been yours since you have the tablet?"

Even though Jim had vouched for Jennifer's abilities, Dylan's face now had a shell-shocked expression and Christopher's was nearly a mirror image of Dylan's.

"Yes," he finally said. "That's exactly where I found it."

"What makes you think Kyle killed Caleb?" Jim asked.

"I didn't see it happen. It was more a vibe I picked up. Kyle is feeling guilty and it's not just about the emails he planted. I'm sure it started before he got the idea to frame Dylan. He's been jealous of you, hasn't he?"

Dylan nodded. "It's because of the way Caleb treated me. I've always tried to look past it and even spoke to Caleb about how Kyle was reacting. I was hoping he wouldn't be as blatant about it so Kyle wouldn't feel bad, but he told me I shouldn't let myself get upset about it. I tried being a friend to Kyle but he pushed me away most of the time unless it would be too obvious to anyone seeing his actions."

"Do you think we should give this information to Phil and Dennis, Jennifer?" Jim asked.

"Are they assigned to this case?"

"They are."

"Wait. Didn't you say you didn't want other people to know about your abilities?" Dylan asked.

"They already do. I've worked with them on four other cases," Jennifer said. "I think that's a good idea, Jim. We should tell them so they can see if this turns out to be Kyle's plan to take attention away from him. Should I call them now?"

Jim looked at Dylan. "It's your call."

Dylan nodded his head as he thought through the pros and cons before coming to a decision. "Would they be discreet?"

"That's been my experience with them. They know they can't accuse anyone based solely on my impressions. It's a clue but they still have to back it up with evidence."

"Okay, let's read them in on this."

Jennifer reached into her purse for her phone and scrolled through her Contacts for the number for Phil Roberts and pushed the Call button.

"Jennifer, this is a surprise. Is something wrong?" he asked.

"Not with me. I have you on Speaker. I'm here with Dylan Johnson and Jim and Christopher Davis. Jim asked me to use my skills about an item relating to the Caleb Mitchell case. I think you and Dennis will want to know what I learned."

"Really? I'd like to hear more. Will you be around for the next hour? I'll need some time to get in touch with Dennis and meet you… Where exactly are you?"

"Yes, I can stay here until you and Dennis arrive. I'm at Dylan Johnson's house. Do you need the address?"

"No, I've got it. I'll be there soon with or without Dennis. We're off duty now so he may have other plans."

"I understand. We'll be here," she said, looking at the others who nodded their affirmation.

True to his word, Phil Roberts arrived with Dennis Smith twenty minutes later.

"We're going to have to put you on the payroll if this keeps up," Dennis teased Jennifer.

"That would be an interesting conversation with HR about my job title," she replied.

"So, what do you have?" Phil asked.

Dylan explained how he'd found the tablet and the emails it contained.

"We'll need an evidence bag and gloves. I have some in my car," Phil said to Dennis. Shortly after, he came back with both and after donning the gloves, started to place the tablet in the bag.

"Wait! I have an idea. Before you do that, I'd like to make a copy of the emails," Dylan said, and held out his hand for the tablet. Dennis looked at him quizzically, but gave it back to Dylan, who took it to his desktop computer and downloaded the messages into a file.

"And your idea is. . .?" Dennis asked when Dylan returned the tablet. This time he finished placing it in the bag and filled in the information to preserve the chain of evidence.

"You have to have the original to turn into evidence. My idea is to replace it with another one exactly like it in the same place I found this one in case Kyle checks to make sure it's there. And if he's planning to incriminate me with it, you'll need to find it in my office after he tells you where it is."

Phil and Dennis nodded their understanding. "Good thinking!" Phil said.

"What did you see when you held it?" Dennis asked Jennifer.

Jennifer repeated her impressions for the detectives.

"This changes everything," Phil said to Dennis.

7

Dennis picked up the conversation to explain. "Earlier today Kyle Mitchell showed us these same emails which he claims to have found on his father's work computer in an encrypted file. You're lucky to have Jennifer in your corner. If we hadn't found out about this information, you would have been our prime suspect."

"Should you let him think that's what you believe?" Jennifer asked. "He may slip up if he thinks you're focusing on Dylan."

"We need to have more evidence to prove he has a motive. Do you have any thoughts on that?" Phil asked.

"I thought about this earlier when I found the tablet. My first guess would be that it's somehow tied to money. As a partner in the firm, I have access to the financial reports but I hadn't been paying close attention to how much Kyle's salary is. I checked earlier this evening, though. I don't know what other income he might have, but his wife doesn't work and he has two young kids. I've been to their house and the lifestyle they live doesn't match Kyle's income."

"Okay, so there might be money problems. Do you suspect that Mr. Mitchell is embezzling from the firm?" Dennis asked.

Dylan considered the possibility. "If he is, he's also in a position to cover his tracks since he's in charge of the financial records. If we suggested a forensic accountant be brought in, that would tip him off."

"Do you think Sarah would be willing to help?" Phil asked Jennifer.

"Sarah?" Dylan questioned, a puzzled look on his face.

"Sarah Pascal. She's one of the ladies in my quilt club and has been a part of solving those four cases I mentioned earlier. Along with Eva Perkins and Annalise Jordan. We're Glen Lake's version of Jessica Fletcher, with a bit of secret sauce thrown in. Her day job, though, is as a cyber security analyst and she has the skills to go through his computer if she has a way to gain access to it, even if it's remotely. Would you be able to authorize that?" Jennifer asked Dylan.

"I think so. I think Amber and Grace would be willing to help if I asked them. They both adored Caleb and want his killer found."

"Should I ask Eva and Annalise if they'd like to be part of this, too?" Jennifer asked the detectives. "We'll be meeting tomorrow night for our quilt club and I can discuss it with them then."

"If they're willing to help, we wouldn't say no," Phil replied, with a smile.

"I'll second that," Dennis said.

"It will surprise me if they refuse, but I'll talk to them about it tomorrow evening at our weekly meeting and let you know. We should probably all meet again to make a plan once we have the team in place," Jennifer suggested, but then something occurred to her. "On second thought, it might be better to keep the group small. There could be information it would be best to not reveal to more people unless or until it is absolutely necessary." She gave the detectives a pointed look.

"Good point," Phil said, understanding immediately that Jennifer was referring to their paranormal abilities. "How about you acting as the representative for the group in the meantime?"

"That should work." Jennifer hadn't realized how tense she was with worry about outing the ladies until her shoulders sank with relief.

"I'll give you my private cell number so you can get in touch with me, Jennifer. Texting is the better option in case I'm in the office. I wouldn't want our conversation to be overheard by Kyle," Dylan said, and Jennifer nodded her understanding.

"That should wrap things up for tonight. Please let us know if you find anything else," Dennis said, standing to leave and the others followed suit.

Jennifer had mixed feelings as she left. The excitement of a new case to solve with her fellow quilters was offset by the disappointment that their investigation might prove her impressions that Kyle Mitchell had killed his father. Before leaving Dylan's house, she made the decision not to wait until the Cozy Quilts Club meeting to ask if the others would like to help. She took out her phone and sent a group text.

> Just met with Phil and Dennis. They asked us to help them with another murder case. Are you on board?

She hadn't even put the car in Drive before her phone began to ping and three texts came through, all with just one word:

> Yes!!

8

Natalie was still awake when Dylan came back into the house and joined her in the living room.

"That was a lot of cars out there. What's going on?" she asked.

Dylan deliberated how much he could say without giving Jennifer's secret away. "It was about Caleb's death. I know I can trust you, but I'm going to say up front that what I tell you has to be kept between you and me. I think Kyle might be trying to set me up."

Natalie's eyes grew round. "You're joking."

"I wish I was. I don't have proof yet that he is, but my gut is telling me I need to be watching my back. You know Kyle has always been jealous of the way Caleb treated me."

Natalie nodded her head.

"I think that's what is behind this but I don't know why he

would go to this extreme. He has to be in a very bad place to think he could get away with it." Dylan then told her about finding the tablet in his credenza and notifying the detectives investigating the case. He left out the part about Jennifer but finished with the detectives' news that Kyle had contacted them to report the alleged emails between Caleb and Dylan.

"But they believe you?" Natalie asked.

"Yes. It wouldn't make sense that I would tell them about finding it if I was actually involved and they saw the logic in that."

"What are they going to do about it?"

"For now, we let Kyle think they're investigating that angle and I keep my mouth shut. I'm not sure if I'm going to be able to act normally around him, but I'm going to have to do my best. The detectives are going to look into where the tablet was sold and follow any leads about that. Hopefully, they'll be able to trace it to Kyle with proof that would hold up in court."

"Do you think they'll be able to do that?"

Dylan nodded. "I do. Jim Davis vouched for them when I asked if he knew them and told me they're good cops who would do their job. After hearing that, I felt okay about telling them all of this and by the time they left, I was feeling even better. We're going to be okay," he said, leveling his eyes on hers and reached out to take her hand, giving it a gentle squeeze.

"I trust you. Let's call it a night. We've both got busy days tomorrow."

CHAPTER SIX: THE CLUB

"So, what's the story?" Eva asked Jennifer when they were all gathered at her dining room table enjoying their potluck dinner. "Hold that thought. Before we get to it, I have to say I think we've outdone ourselves with this week's choices. I thought using squash as the theme might be as hard as the strawberry week. Not using pumpkin was a good idea, too. We'll have enough of that at the end of the month or even sooner if you're into pumpkin spice. That seems to be everywhere these days. Sarah, I had to use all my self-control to stop eating the zucchini bites so I didn't fill up on them and ruin the rest of my meal. And that garlic dip adds just the right touch."

"Thanks, Eva. I made a practice batch and Ashley and I pigged out on them so I thought they might be a hit. Annalise, this squash casserole is delicious. I've never had it before and would love to have the recipe. Ashley and I are trying to add more vegetarian meals to our diet," Sarah said.

"Thanks, Sarah. It's one of those dishes that could be used either for the entrée or a side dish."

"I would never have thought of using butternut squash for

bread, but this turned out really well, if I do say so myself," Jennifer said. "I'm glad we talked about what to make to go with the casserole, Annalise."

"It's delicious!" Sarah said, reaching for another slice, but stopped when Eva brought a plate of cookies to the table that she'd placed on the buffet earlier. "Speaking of saving my appetite!"

"Are the pumpkin cookies from a family recipe, Eva? They remind me of cookies my mother made when I was growing up," Annalise asked.

"Yes, it's my grandmother's recipe. Some people don't care for the raisins and nuts, but I like the flavor and the texture they add."

"I'd love to have the recipe if you're willing to share," Jennifer said.

"Of course. I'll make a copy right now so I don't forget."

"Would you make a copy for me, too, please?" Sarah asked.

"And while you're at it…" Annalise said, smiling.

Eva returned her smile. "Three copies coming right up."

She returned several minutes later and handed a copy to each of them.

"Now, Jennifer, I'm dying to hear what happened at Dylan's."

The others listened attentively as Jennifer told them what had happened the evening before at Dylan's house and her offer to Phil and Dennis for the Club to assist with the investigation.

"Does Dylan know what it is we do?" Sarah asked.

"He knows about my psychometry, of course, but I didn't mention the skills each of you have. I was able to skirt around it when I asked Phil and Dennis about including all of us to help. I told Dylan we assisted them with other cases, but not how. I'm surprised he didn't ask more questions but I think he was still processing the information I'd given him about the tablet. We left it that I would be the representative for all of us. If Dylan discovers Kyle has been embezzling from the firm, having Sarah do a deep dive into Kyle's financial information wouldn't raise any eyebrows. If you want to try contacting Caleb, though, we'd need to have access to the office. Dylan could let you in after hours, but it would mean explaining why and what you would be doing." She hesitated. "How do you all feel about that?" she asked them.

"Let's cross that bridge if and when we come to it. It might not even be necessary if there's enough other evidence to arrest him for the murder."

"I can't think of anything I can do to help this time, at least with my animal whispering skills, so it probably won't come up. If Dylan asked about how I helped with the other cases, though, I wouldn't want to lie but I'm not completely comfortable with admitting I got the information from a dog and a cat. This is a small town and it wouldn't take long before everyone knew about it. I'm not sure if I'm ready to deal with it."

"That's understandable. We're not actually Dylan's clients, so even though the rules about confidentiality wouldn't apply, I think he could be trusted. If we can help without revealing our secrets, that seems like the best route to take," Annalise said.

"Okay, are we all on board then?" Jennifer asked.

Eva nodded. "Yes, if I can help, I'm happy to do so."

"Me, too. I'll try a meditation later to see if anything comes up," Annalise said.

Sarah was the last to reply. "You've all made good points. I don't have any concerns about helping and like you said, Jennifer, we can deal with whether or not to contact Caleb if we need to. If Dylan needs it, please give him my contact information."

"Thank you, everyone. I should have asked before offering everyone's help but it just slipped out in my excitement to help out with another case."

Eva reached out and patted Jennifer's hand. "Don't fret about it. There's no harm done and I'm glad you did ask us. Now that we've got that settled, how about we do what we really came here for? Quilting!"

"Sounds good to me! Let's clear the table and tidy up the kitchen. I haven't had a chance all week to work on my project, and I can't wait to start sewing," Annalise said.

CHAPTER SEVEN: SARAH & DYLAN

Jennifer texted Dylan the next morning to give him the news that the Club was ready to help whenever he gave the word. She didn't have to wait long for a reply.

> Would you please give Sarah my number and have her text me? I'd like to set up a meeting with her at my house ASAP to discuss the forensic accounting.

> I'll do that right now.

Jennifer started composing a new text, but decided to call instead. "Hi, Sarah. Dylan Johnson would like to meet to talk about doing the forensic accounting for the law firm. He asked if you would send him a text rather than call, though. He has client meetings throughout the day so a text wouldn't interrupt him and he'd rather not have you leave a message with his personal assistant."

"Sure. Give me a sec to open my contacts." She picked up her phone and began a new Contact entry for Dylan Johnson. "Okay, I'm ready. What's his number?"

"It's 555-2813 and he lives at 23 Sinclair Drive. Would you like me to go with you?"

"No, I think I'll be fine on my own. You've already given him my name and what I do and, at least for now, he doesn't need to know anything about my ghost whispering. If that does come up at some point, I might need you to vouch for me."

"Understood. If you change your mind, just let me know. It's no problem."

"Thanks, Jen."

As soon as they'd disconnected the call, Sarah debated putting off contacting Dylan until later. She had a project she needed to work on, but decided it would be better to just get this chore off her to do list sooner than later. Heeding the request for a text rather than a phone call, she typed in a message and hit the send arrow.

> Hi, Dylan. This is Sarah Pascal. Jennifer Ryder let me know you'd like to set up an appointment with me.

> Thanks for getting back so quickly. Can you meet me tonight at 6:30?

Sarah checked her calendar to make sure she didn't already have a commitment she'd forgotten about.

> I can do that. Jennifer gave me your address, so I'm set with that.

> Great! See you tonight!

> Almost forgot. I have a home office above the garage. You get to it through the doorway next to the garage bays. I'll keep an ear out for you.

Sarah replied with the thumbs up emoji.

2

It was dark by the time she arrived at Dylan's house, a two-story colonial located in one of the newer subdivisions of Glen Lake. The driveway was empty but Sarah assumed the cars were parked inside the attached garage. She went to the door where Dylan had told her to come in, unsure whether she should just go in or ring the doorbell, when she heard footsteps descending a stairway. The door opened and she was greeted by a man in his late thirties or early forties. He was tall, blonde, and attractive but Sarah noticed a strained look around his eyes. Considering what she'd been told by Jennifer about his current situation, she wasn't surprised.

"Sarah?"

She smiled and nodded in acknowledgement.

"Come on in. My office is upstairs."

To their left was another door which entered into the garage but the stairway had been separated from the area where the cars were stored, and sheet-rocked to give it a finished appearance. He led the way up to his home office which was decorated in dark colors and simple furnishings. Only a bare minimum of woven textured pillows adorned the leather couch and chairs in the sitting area of the room's open floor plan. Sarah took note of the espresso-colored desk facing toward them with only a desktop computer, what looked like a tablet device, and the backs of photo frames which undoubtedly held pictures of his wife and children occupying the desk's surface. Built-in bookcases behind the desk contained a broad mix of fiction and non-fiction books, although the fiction leaned toward mysteries and suspense. Abstract paintings on the walls provided some pops of color to the otherwise solid colors in the room. Despite its minimalist esthetic, Sarah felt a warm sensation when she entered the space and attributed it to Dylan himself. Her sensitivity had enabled her to feel the presence of ghosts and also to judge the character of the living. The positive vibes Dylan was emanating put her at ease even before they began talking and she knew she could trust what he told her.

"Have a seat," he said gesturing toward one of the two overstuffed leather chairs and waited until she was seated before sitting on the couch facing Sarah. "Did Jennifer give you the back story of why I asked you to come tonight?"

"She told us about the incriminating emails on the tablet you discovered and that you're guessing it was planted in your office by Kyle Mitchell. And you're wondering if I could search through his financial records to see if there's anything out of the ordinary going on with those. Am I understanding that correctly?"

"Yes. At least partly. I'd like you to examine the firm's financial records as well. Kyle is the office manager and controls the books which will make it more difficult especially since I don't want to tip him off that I suspect he's trying to frame me because he killed Caleb."

"Does that mean you don't have access yourself to any of the records?"

"That's correct. As a full partner, I get copies of the reports he prepares but I've never asked him for access to the accounts themselves."

"Could you do that without clueing him in that you're suspicious?"

"I'm not sure." Dylan looked away as he thought about the question and then his expression became animated. "I can't believe I didn't think about this sooner. Grace Foster is our paralegal and she's been handling the paperwork for probate. She would need to have that information for various filings. I can ask her to get it for me."

"Does she have authority to access the accounts virtually or would she only have the account numbers?"

"She might only have the bank statements that Kyle prints off for her." Dylan's shoulders slumped as his excitement left as quickly as it had arrived.

"Do you think she would be willing to approach Kyle about it if she isn't already an authorized user? Maybe she could make up an excuse that she needs it for the probate. I have no idea what that could be but the two of you might."

"If she doesn't have permission already, I'll ask her to go through the statements first to see if there are any expenditures that don't appear to be legitimate. It wouldn't hurt to have her compare billing statements to make sure they match the time sheets we've submitted. He could have been skimming off the payments we've received. It might save you some time if she sees anything off just by examining those."

"Can you count on her to keep this between the two of you? We wouldn't want to tip Kyle off before we can do a more thorough review. He could alter the records to cover his tracks. He's probably been doing that already but if he thought he was under suspicion, he'd make a point of fabricating ironclad documentation."

"That's why I've asked you to help. From what I've been told, you have the skills to find the evidence even if he has."

"I appreciate the vote of confidence, but I can't guarantee I will. But even if I don't, you can be sure that I've tried my best. I had another thought about the tablet. Would you like me to follow up on that? I can get in touch with Phil and Dennis to make sure they're okay if I do, but it might save some time tracing the purchase and how Kyle planted the email chain. My understanding is that they they had to take it to put into evidence, but you've made a copy of the emails."

"That's correct. I thought you might need those so I've already made a copy on a flash drive for you."

He went to his desk and retrieved the flash drive and handed it to her.

"Perfect. Yes, I can use that to get started."

She paused to weigh her words before making her next request. "Are you willing to allow me to use more clandestine methods if it becomes necessary? And to back me up later if I have to reveal my methods for gathering the information?"

He held her gaze as the meaning behind the words sunk in.

"Yes, and yes."

CHAPTER EIGHT: DYLAN AND GRACE

Grace reached for her phone when she heard the ping of an incoming text. *That's odd,* she thought when she read the text from Dylan asking her to come to his office. *Why didn't he just come up to talk to her? Guess I'll find out when I get there,* she answered her own question and sent a text back telling him she'd be right down.

"Close the door, please," he told her when she walked into his office.

She did as he asked but her brows knit together in confusion. This wasn't typical.

"What's up?" she asked after taking a seat in one of the client chairs facing Dylan.

"How is it going with Caleb's probate paperwork?"

Grace was still confused. The request wasn't matching the drama of Dylan's behavior. *Something else is going on here.*

"It's on schedule. The preliminary paperwork has been filed and the Will submitted for probate. It took a little longer than usual to receive a death certificate because of the circumstances but not a big deal. What are you really asking? I have the feeling this isn't the only reason you called me in."

Dylan smiled, relieving some of the tension in the room.

"Can't get anything by you, can I? What I'm about to ask you to do has to remain strictly between you and me. Can you do that?"

"Without knowing what it is, I'm not sure I'm willing to answer that. On the other hand, I've known you for ten years and you've never asked me to do anything illegal or shady, so I'll say yes. I can keep it between us."

"I want you to go through all of the firm's financials for our primary account and the escrow account. Also look through our accounts receivable. Check the time sheets for billing for all three of us and compare them to the amount billed to the client and our calendars to make sure those add up. You should go back through the last twelve months to start. Look for any unusual expenditures. Do you have permission to access the firm's bank accounts or does it all go through Kyle?"

"It's funny you should ask. About a month ago Caleb took me aside and told me he wanted me to go with him to the bank. He added me as an authorized signatory with permission to set up an online username so I could audit the accounts. He told me he didn't want Kyle to know I could do that. Did he say something to you before he died about thinking Kyle might be dipping into the accounts?"

Now it was Dylan's turn to be confused.

"No, he didn't say anything to me. I can't tell you all of what's going on yet. I'd like to wait until you've had a chance to go through the records in case my suspicions are off base. Although..." He paused, looking away as he considered. "If Caleb suspected something before he died to the point that he asked you to be on the accounts, it might be more than my imagination," he said more to himself than Grace. He looked back at her, having made his decision. "On second thought, I'm going to put you in touch with a woman named Sarah Pascal. I've been in touch with her about doing a forensic accounting. Kyle's behavior recently has been off and I think he's going through some money problems. You've seen the renovations he and Erica made when they had everyone at their Fourth of July party. That had to have cost a small fortune."

"It looked like a page right out of a magazine. I probably shouldn't talk about her behind her back, but Erica comes across as a shopper. That must cause some issues, too." Grace said.

"You're saying out loud what we're all thinking. Caleb must have either known or suspected Kyle was having problems."

"I'll do whatever I can to help Sarah and keep it on the down low. For his sake, I hope we don't find anything," Grace said.

I wouldn't bet on it, is what he didn't say. Instead, he replied, "Me, too."

CHAPTER NINE: SARAH AND GRACE

1

"Hello, Grace. This is Sarah Pascal. Dylan Johnson suggested I call you about your firm's financials. Is this a good time?"

"Let me just close my door first."

She put the call on Hold and walked to her door where she could see Kyle's office directly opposite. He appeared to be absorbed in his work and didn't even look up. She closed her door softly before returning to her desk.

"Thank you for holding. Kyle's office is opposite mine and it's an old building."

"I understand. Would it be possible for you to come to my office instead so you could speak more freely?" Sarah asked.

"That's an excellent idea. I don't have any appointments this morning. Would that work for you?"

"Absolutely. Here's my address."

Grace typed the address into her Contacts on her phone. "I should be there in twenty minutes." She disconnected the call and leaned over to put her laptop in the messenger bag underneath her desk. She pushed back her chair and picked up the messenger bag and her purse and was about to leave when she looked up and saw Kyle in her doorway staring at her. Her cheeks flushed and her stomach clenched but she smiled hoping she didn't appear as flustered as she felt.

"Kyle. You startled me. I didn't even hear my door open."

"Sorry, I should have knocked first. Are you going out?" He looked pointedly at her purse and bag.

"Yes. I have some papers to file at the courthouse. Is there something you need?"

He leveled his gaze at her and held it briefly. Grace held her breath but kept her eyes on his.

"It's not important." He turned and walked back toward his office.

Grace blew out her breath slowly through her mouth and waited for her heart to stop hammering in her chest before grabbing her coat and walking down the front stairs. She'd planned to use the back stairway but it would mean walking by Kyle's office. She stopped at Amber's office first.

"I need to be out for about an hour, maybe two."

"Are you okay?" Amber asked. "You look as though you're upset."

"I'm fine. I must still be thinking about the case I'm working on. Gotta go." She smiled at Amber and gave her a wave, walking out before she could ask any more questions. As she was walking toward her car she felt a tingle up her spine and looked up. She inhaled sharply when she saw Kyle looking down at her from his office window. Recovering, she smiled at him and picked up her pace. She backed her car out of its spot and glanced up at Kyle's window as she drove past, but he wasn't there. Still shaken, she pulled out of the driveway and onto the road into Bangor.

2

"Did you have any trouble finding me?" Sarah asked.

"Not a bit. My GPS brought me straight here," Grace said as she walked into the entry of Sarah's house.

Sarah's attention was drawn upward as the sound of scratching and whimpering flowed down the stairway.

"That's my dog, Max. Are you okay with dogs? I promise he's a sweetheart, but if you're allergic or are uncomfortable around them, I can put him in another room."

"I love dogs. It's no problem at all."

"Can I get you anything before we go upstairs to my office? Water? Tea or coffee?"

"No, I'm all set, but thank you."

"In that case, let's get to it."

Sarah led the way to her office. As soon as she opened the door, a golden retriever bounded out, his tail wagging so vigorously that his back end was wagging along with it. He gave Sarah a quick glance as though to say thank you for opening the door and then immediately went to Grace and sniffed her hand. She rewarded him by stroking his head.

"He's so soft!"

"He had a spa day yesterday at the groomer's. Didn't you, Max?" He looked up at her with his big, brown eyes and responded with a woof! "Okay, now that you've met Grace, we're going to get to work. Go lay down on your bed."

He hesitated and turned to Grace again, but trotted to the dog bed in Sarah's office when Sarah walked into her office with Grace following behind. He circled his dog bed three times before settling down with his chin resting on his front paws, looking up at the women as they sat at Sarah's desk.

"Dylan told me that you would have the firm's banking information including the passwords for the accounts. I realize it was only yesterday when he spoke with you, but have you had a chance to look for any anomalies in the deposits and with-drawals?"

"Not in depth yet but I have pulled together the reports for the firm's billing and time sheets. I have them on my laptop." She put the messenger bag on her lap and pulled out the device. After it had booted up, she opened the file with the reports and turned it around so Sarah could see the screen.

"Do you mind if I put this on a flash drive?"

"Not at all. Dylan told me I should share with you whatever you need. Before you do that, let me pull up the file with the bank account information and the pin number for the two-factor authentication so you can download it at the same time."

After Sarah had transferred the data to her drive, she plugged it into her own computer so they could view it on her monitor.

"I didn't get this put together until late yesterday afternoon after Dylan spoke to me. I found an inconsistency between the time sheets and the client invoices for last month's billing, but haven't had time to go back more than that."

They spent the next forty-five minutes examining the reports and found additional discrepancies in which several clients had been billed more than the time sheets Dylan, Grace, and Caleb had turned in. Grace checked her watch and was surprised at how much time had gone by.

"I'm going to need to get back to the office. I told Amber I'd only be gone an hour or two. Do you have enough information to keep looking through the books?"

"I think so. I should be able to log into the accounts without triggering any alerts to Kyle. I have a few trade secrets I can use to avoid that." Sarah grinned at Grace who grinned back, under-standing what she wasn't saying.

"In that case, I'll leave you to it. If you need anything else, though, here's my private cell number so you can text me. That way there won't be any opportunity for eavesdropping." She told Sarah about Kyle's behavior before she'd left the office.

Sarah frowned. "Be careful. If Kyle is responsible in any way, even if it's just about embezzlement, he could be dangerous if he feels threatened."

Grace bit her lip. "I thought about that all the way here. I know Dylan asked me to do this with your help, but after what happened, I think it would be better if you're the one digging into this. I'm happy to help if you need anything, but it's a small office and I'm not a very good liar. If Kyle confronted me, I'm afraid I might slip up."

"I get that and agree with you one hundred percent about staying out of this. I'll speak to Dylan myself about what you've told me."

"Thanks!" Grace's shoulders relaxed and the relief was visible on her face. "It was a pleasure meeting you. And you, too, Max," she said as she leaned down to pat the sleeping dog's head. He opened one eye to gaze up at her and then sighed and went back to sleep, content to stay behind as the women walked downstairs.

3

Grace was relieved to see that Kyle's car wasn't in the parking lot when she returned to the office. She'd been dreading seeing him again during the drive back from Sarah's house. She opted to go in the back way and went immediately to Dylan's office, knocking softly before entering and then closing the door behind her. He looked up from his computer and gave her a concerned look.

"Are you okay?"

"Yes. I had an uncomfortable interaction with Kyle earlier today and was worried about seeing him." She told him about the incident with Kyle. "It made me think that it might be better for Sarah to continue looking into the accounts on her own. I just met with her before coming in to speak with you."

"Does she have everything she'll need to keep investigating?"

"She should, but I told her if she needed anything else to call me. I'm probably blowing this all out of proportion and Kyle's behavior might not have had anything to do with this. It could be I have a guilty conscience and he doesn't have a clue that I'm looking into the firm's accounts more than I should be for the probate, but I'd feel better…"

"No need to explain. I agree it's better to let Sarah do this. It's imperative that we don't let on we suspect him."

Grace let out a deep breath. "You have no idea how relieved I am to hear you say that."

"Considering how worried you looked when you came in, I have a feeling I do."

"Alright, then, I think I'm going to call it a day. I think now I might actually be able to sleep tonight."

"You do that. I'll see you tomorrow."

She gathered up her messenger bag and purse and walked toward the front of the building to let Amber know she was leaving. She was so focused on getting her car keys out of her purse that she didn't notice Kyle in the hallway. It was only his outstretched hand that kept her from plowing into him and she let out a squeak when she felt it on her shoulder.

"You scared the daylights out of me!"

"Sorry, Grace. It looked like you didn't see me." He smiled but she noticed it didn't reach his eyes.

"You're right, I didn't. I was looking for my keys," she said, holding them up. "I didn't realize you were in the office. Your car wasn't in the driveway when I got back."

There was an awkward moment when he didn't reply and was blocking her path.

"Um… I was about to leave for the day and wanted to let Amber know," she said, moving forward enough that he was forced to step aside. "Goodnight. I'll see you tomorrow!"

"Yeah, tomorrow," he replied and she felt his eyes on her

back as she walked away. When she reached Amber's office she couldn't help herself from looking back but he was no longer standing there.

CHAPTER TEN: KYLE

The creditors had given him a reprieve after he reassured them he would soon be receiving an inheritance and could bring his accounts back to current status. The argument he'd had with Erica had been the worst they'd ever had. When he told her he'd cancelled their credit cards and insisted she give him back the ones she had, and then cut them up in front of her, she'd begun berating him for being a lousy provider. He'd surprised even himself when he countered that by telling her *she* was the problem, not him. If she didn't spend half her time shopping on needless things and renovating a house that was perfectly fine before that, they wouldn't be in this mess. He hadn't intended to, but to put an exclamation point on his accusation, he grabbed the stack of credit card statements and delinquent notices on their mortgage from the counter where he'd put them, and taking her hand, shoved them into it. She tried to make him take them back but he refused. And then he insisted that she look at each of them while he waited, seething with anger. At first she barely glanced at the statement on the top of the pile, angrily putting it to the bottom of the others. As she worked her way through them, more slowly with each one, and the reality of their situation and her part in it sunk in, her shoulders slumped. When she looked up at Kyle again, her eyes were brimming with tears.

It was a subdued Erica who said, "I'm sorry, Kyle. I had no idea. Why didn't you talk to me about this before?"

He snorted. "As if I could. And don't you think I've tried? Whenever I would bring up not spending so much money, you would throw a temper tantrum and for the next two or three days you'd sulk and give me the cold shoulder. After a while, I just gave up. It wasn't worth the attitude I'd get from you."

"That's not true. I wouldn't..." In a rare moment of self-realization, Erica stopped arguing. "You're absolutely right. I did do that. I'm sorry I was such a spoiled brat."

"It's not completely your fault. Your parents let you get away with that all your life."

She nodded her head. "Yes, they did, but I'm an adult now. I need to start acting like one."

After that, they had a heart-to-heart discussion about how they would pull themselves out of debt. When he brought up his inheritance from Caleb, her face brightened and he knew exactly what she was thinking.

"No, Erica. Don't even think about it. This isn't a short-term solution so that you can go back to spending my salary like it's coming off a money tree."

He thought he saw the beginning of a pout on her face and was afraid she would try to manipulate him like she always had. He stared back at her, his eyes level with hers and his expression unrelenting. She nodded her head at last, knowing this time he wouldn't back down.

I wish I'd done this years ago, but better late than never.

For the first time in a long time, he slept like a baby, until he woke with a start, sitting upright.

Kyle, be a man and admit what you've done.

It had to have been a dream, but he'd heard the voice so clearly. Caleb's voice.

CHAPTER ELEVEN: THE CLUB

"Grace Foster and I met yesterday," Sarah told the Club at their weekly meeting. "I suggested we meet at my house because she was concerned about Kyle overhearing her."

"Oh, I like Grace! She's got a good head on her shoulders and she was very loyal to Caleb," Eva said.

"I got that same impression. She was able to give me the information I'll need to dig into the firm's finances to see if Dylan's suspicions are founded. Grace hadn't had time to do an in-depth examination, but she found some discrepancies with the billing so I'd be surprised if there isn't more going on. I had another project I needed to work on today but tomorrow I'm making Mitchell & Johnson my priority."

"I'm so disappointed with all of this. It has completely altered my opinion of Kyle. I'd never have thought he would embezzle from the firm, much less kill Caleb," Jennifer said.

"The vibe I'm getting is that there's more going on with Kyle. I don't have any clear visions about what that is, though," Annalise said.

"He's made Grace uncomfortable recently. She said he was

lurking around her office and she thought he might have been eavesdropping on her conversation with me."

"That tracks with what's coming through to me," Annalise agreed.

There was a lull in the conversation.

"Moving on to a different topic, this might be a good time to bring up some news I heard," Annalise said.

"Let me guess. You were eating at the Diner," Eva joked.

Annalise chuckled. "You've got it in one! Betty told me the town Rec Department is organizing a holiday craft fair. They're using it as a fundraiser for the summer recreation program so there's a fee to rent a table, but it's only twenty-five dollars, and they're going to do an auction so they're soliciting donations for that, too. I thought it would be fun if we all shared a table."

"I'll need to check my schedule to make sure I'd be available. When would it be?" Sarah asked.

"They're planning it for three weekends beginning with the Thanksgiving weekend, but you could do however many as you're able. If all four of us contributed, we should have enough items to fill the table and there would be time in between to make more to replace what we've sold. I wouldn't mind covering for you if you can't do all three events," Annalise offered.

"That sounds like fun. I'm in," Eva said. "And I just happen to have a stash of holiday themed designs that I would love to share with everyone. Although those new fabrics they got in at Quilting Essentials are still calling to me."

"Don't do it, Eva!" Annalise said, sternly. "Remember our pact?"

Eva's face fell and her shoulders slumped. "I do," she said and sighed. "But they're so pretty."

"Don't give me those puppy dog eyes. I'm doing this for your own good," Annalise said, her voice still firm, but they both knew it was put on.

Sarah and Jennifer looked on with amusement.

"I'd love to have some of your stash. I haven't made anything holiday-themed before so I don't have any fabric like that," Sarah said. "What kind of things would you make for this?"

"Oh, it doesn't have to be anything big or time-consuming," Jennifer said, warming to the subject. "People are looking for things they can give as gifts as well as use themselves. So, placemat sets, wine bags, tree skirts, mug rugs, and wall hangings are perfect for craft fairs."

"It should come as no surprise that I just happen to have a book with holiday projects if you need some inspiration, Sarah," Eva said.

"That would be great! Thanks, Eva."

"Glad I can help. Should we each choose something or just make whatever appeals to us?" Eva asked the group.

"I think it would be okay if we made whatever we would like. Between the four of us we should be able to come up with enough things to sell. Even if we all made placemats, the chances are good they would all come out differently. We've got time between now and then to figure it out," Jennifer said.

"It sounds like everyone is on board. Should I apply for a table?" Annalise asked.

Three heads nodded.

Eva clapped her hands excitedly. "This is going to be so much fun! Let me get that box of fabrics and we can pick out what we want so we can get started. I'm close to being done with the coin quilt and honestly, I'm ready to start something new. Whose idea was it to do a coin quilt, anyway?"

"Yours!" the others said in unison, their faces beaming.

Busted!

Eva looked down to see Reuben staring up at her, a smug expression on his face.

CHAPTER TWELVE: SARAH & DYLAN

A week had passed before Sarah examined Kyle's financial accounts and had enough information to contact Dylan.

"I have information you're going to want to see. It would be easier for me if you come to my house so I can use my computer and there wouldn't be any chance the wrong people see it."

Dylan felt a twinge of regret. The tone of Sarah's voice told him she would be confirming the inconsistencies Grace had found. He'd hoped Sarah would discover an explanation for them that didn't prove Kyle was stealing from the firm. They set up a time and Sarah gave Dylan her address.

As soon as he opened the door to the enclosed porch, he heard a dog barking, getting louder as it approached from the opposite side. Sarah had warned him about her dog, Max. In her words, his bark was much worse than his bite, so it didn't worry him but even so, the butterflies in his stomach began to fly. Sarah opened the door, holding onto Max's collar with one hand.

"It's okay, Max. He's a friend."

Max looked at her briefly and then focused on Dylan, but stopped barking and sniffed at his hand before giving it a lick.

His long feathery tail was wagging, putting Dylan at ease once again.

"Come on in, Dylan. If you're okay, I'll let Max go now. Don't let those puppy dog eyes trick you. If he could get away with it, he'd be begging for your attention the entire time you're here."

"I'm okay," Dylan said, and kneeled down to Max's level, stroking him behind his ears, ruffling his fur. Max took it in with blissful appreciation. "You be a good boy. Your mom and I have some business to attend to." Dylan gave him one last pat on the head and stood up. As though Max had understood what he'd been told, he turned and trotted off to the back of the house.

"Ashley, Dylan Johnson is here now. We're going up to my office," Sarah called out to her wife who was out of sight, but then walked out from the back of the house to greet them.

"Hi, I'm Ashley Donovan," she said, extending her hand to Dylan.

"Nice to meet you, Ashley. I'm sorry to horn in on your time with Sarah but I hope it won't take too long and the two of you can enjoy the rest of your evening."

"Don't worry about it. I'm used to Sarah working odd hours," she said, giving Dylan a warm smile. "I have some work of my own to do and this will force me to do it instead of watching TV."

"My office is upstairs," Sarah said, leading the way. "Why don't you pull up one of the chairs so you can see my screen?" she told him once they were in her office.

"I take it that you've found something or I wouldn't be here," Dylan said.

"I'm afraid so. I'll start with my report documenting where Kyle bought the tablet and proof that the emails on Caleb's computer and the tablet were faked. It doesn't conclusively prove that he was the one who put them there, but the fact that he bought it and I was able to trace the serial number to that purchase is circumstantial evidence. It might be enough for the detectives to get him to confess."

Dylan nodded, his eyes reflecting his sadness. "I would never have imagined Kyle's jealousy of me going to this extreme. What happened to make him do this?" he said so quietly Sarah had to listen closely to hear.

Knowing it was a rhetorical question, she opened another file on her screen. "This is my report on Kyle's personal finances. Quite honestly, I don't know how he's been able to keep from having to declare bankruptcy. He has five credit cards with credit limits between five to twenty-five thousand on each and he owes about sixty thousand dollars on those. They aren't maxed out, but they're close. I'm guessing he's made sure to have some credit on each so he and his wife can still use them. He only made a minimum payment on all of them last month, but even that is a lot when you add them all together. He has both a first and second mortgage on his home and is behind on the payments. The last two months, he's gone into the grace period or I'm sure they would have begun foreclosure proceedings already. He's juggling payments between the two of them so they never go two months behind. His savings account, the one that is a joint account with his wife, Erica, has a balance of less than a thousand dollars and their checking account is about the same." Sarah paused to give Dylan time to absorb what she'd told him.

He remained quiet, digesting this news. "No wonder he's been so tense lately. I'm guessing this isn't the whole story, though. Has he been dipping into the firm's accounts to stay afloat?"

"Yes. He's done a reasonably good job of covering his tracks, so it took some digging to find how he's doing it. I looked through each of the accounts payable expenditures and one turned out to be a nonexistent company. He's been creating bills for a software subscription service and sending them payments of five hundred dollars a month. It's not much, which was probably smart, because it wouldn't immediately raise red flags if there was an audit. I didn't recognize the company and when I dug deeper, I discovered the only client for this company was your firm. The payments have been deposited in a bank account he opened online. Kyle must have forged the paperwork to make it look like a legitimate business. He's the sole account holder and he withdraws cash from it using an ATM. It doesn't get deposited to his other bank accounts so my guess is he uses that for things like groceries, gas for his car, that sort of thing. Still, it doesn't seem like that would be enough motive for him to worry about if he was caught. Certainly not enough to kill his father over."

Dylan nodded. "I agree. Caleb would have been furious if he found out and he might have fired Kyle but he wouldn't have pressed charges."

"I had an idea about what might have happened, but the only way to prove it is to ask Kyle directly. Do you think he might have asked Caleb for the money to cover his debts? And if he did, would Caleb have given it to him?"

Dylan considered that scenario. "I suppose that's possible. Caleb could be hard-nosed, especially with Kyle. From what you've told me about his circumstances, Kyle might have asked out of desperation. Caleb left him his house and a hundred thousand dollars in his Will. That would have been enough to bring him out of debt. Still… to kill Caleb to get it? I can't imagine that, but I know what desperation can do to people."

"So where does this leave us?"

"This information should be turned over to Phil and Dennis and let them take it to wherever it leads."

Dylan sighed. "It's not what I want to do, but you're absolutely right."

CHAPTER THIRTEEN: THE CLUB

The four quilters were enjoying their dessert and coffee following the potluck dinner at their regular meeting before the conversation turned to the investigation of Caleb Mitchell's murder.

"Were you able to find anything confirming Kyle Mitchell had been embezzling from the firm?" Jennifer asked Sarah.

"I did. Dylan came to my house last night and I gave him the report. He's going to give a copy to Phil and Dennis to follow up with. He was able to provide me with the access to the firm's accounts without letting Kyle know he was doing it because their paralegal, Grace, is doing the probate work. I have to admit Kyle was clever about how he hid it, but he was no match for Super Sleuth Sarah." She gave them all a wide grin.

"Is that your official title now?" Eva asked, chuckling.

"I might just do it as a cross-stitch project and have it framed to hang over my desk. If only I knew how," Sarah replied. She went on to tell them in more detail how she had discovered the phony business and bank account Kyle had set up.

"This is probably a good time to bring up what I've learned," Annalise said, and the ladies gave her their full attention. "I finally had the chance to do a meditation and tuned into Kyle. I'm convinced he wasn't just embezzling from the firm. I believe he is the one who killed Caleb. The guilt and strain of keeping his secret is getting to him and he's beginning to unravel. It's possible Caleb's spirit is playing a part as well. I don't think he's crossed over yet and is haunting Kyle. You might have to do an intervention, Sarah. I don't know how to do that without revealing that you're a ghost whisperer, though. Unless anyone can think of a reason why Sarah could have access to Caleb's office alone."

Sarah sighed. "I was afraid it might come to that. I haven't been contacted by Caleb directly but I've had the sensation of a presence around me while I was looking into Kyle's finances. If I can avoid it, I'd rather not let anyone else into the circle of people who know about my abilities. It isn't that I don't trust Dylan, because I do." The others waited while she processed her next thought. "Okay, now that I've said that out loud, I feel better about letting Dylan in. What do you think, Annalise? Is this urgent or can we wait to see how things play out now that Phil and Dennis know Kyle had a motive to kill Caleb in order to get his inheritance sooner?"

"I didn't have a sense of urgency but my gut feeling is that an intervention will have to happen eventually so that Caleb can move on."

Sarah only nodded her understanding and her earlier playfulness had disappeared.

"That's a somber note to end on, but why don't we take our minds off the subject and go to our sewing stations? There's nothing like some quilt therapy to take me to my happy place," Eva suggested.

"I couldn't agree more!" Jennifer chimed in.

Annalise patted Sarah's shoulder as she passed by on her way to the sewing studio. "You know you've got us standing by you no matter what, right?"

Sarah looked up and gave Annalise a wry smile. "I do. Like Eva said, a little quilt therapy and I'll feel better." The two women walked together to the sewing room, the bond of belonging to a group that had each other's backs stronger than ever.

CHAPTER FOURTEEN: KYLE

Kyle was dragging. He'd never gotten back to sleep after his dream and hearing Caleb's voice so clearly. He didn't believe in ghosts, but it had seemed so… *real*. He'd been tempted to call in sick but thought better of it. This might be the day that the detectives came to arrest Dylan or, at the very least, take him in for questioning. It had been two days since he'd told them about the tablet, which reminded him, he should check to make sure it was still in the credenza after everyone left for the day. If Dylan had found it, he hadn't said anything.

He came into the office through the rear door so he could grab a cup of coffee and take the back stairs to his office. He wasn't in the mood for socializing this morning. He put the cup on his desk and was sitting down when his monitor came awake, immediately catching his attention because he was sure he'd turned his computer off last night. His mouth gaped open and his knees buckled. Had his chair not been directly behind him, he would have fallen to the floor. Filling the screen, typed in 24-point font, repeated over and over again were the words

Be a man, Kyle. Admit what you've done.

CHAPTER FIFTEEN: SARAH

Annalise's suggestion that she might have to confess to Dylan that she could speak to ghosts had been on Sarah's mind ever since last night. With the exception of Detectives Smith and Roberts, the only people who knew her secret were close friends, and Ashley, of course. Had it not been necessary in order to convince them she had information that would lead to the arrest of a killer in the Cozy Quilts Club's previous cases, the detectives wouldn't know either. At first they thought she was putting them on, but had come to accept it wasn't a parlor trick. Jim was in on her secret, too, and she assumed that if he vouched for her, Dylan would at least give her the benefit of the doubt.

She thought about how to bring it up. Leading with *Oh, by the way, could you take me to Caleb's office after hours? I'd like to speak to his ghost. He might be able to tell us what happened the night he died,* didn't strike her as the best approach. She wasn't sure the detectives would be the best choice to broach the subject either. Even though they accepted she really could communicate with the dead, Sarah didn't think they would be comfortable admitting to anyone outside the small circle the Club had formed, that they had trusted her information to close their cases.

Jim, then? He didn't have as much to lose as the detectives would, so that was a possibility. She'd give him a call later to ask. With that decision made, she was finally able to relax.

"I think I figured it out, Max," she said.

He was sleeping on his bed pulled up close to her desk but opened one eye and sighed in delight as his human stroked his head just the way he liked it. Sarah returned her attention to the project she'd been working on for her day job and Max fell back to sleep, snoring softly, both feeling all was right with the world.

CHAPTER SIXTEEN: KYLE

"Was somebody in my father's office?" Kyle asked Amber, storming into her office.

She jumped at his sharp tone.

"I… I don't think so," she replied.

Caleb's office door had been shut since the crime scene investigators had finished their search for clues. It hadn't been a decision they'd discussed as a group, but the unspoken understanding was that everyone preferred to keep it closed. Kyle had only gone into the room to retrieve a file.

"Are you sure?"

"Well, I suppose somebody could have gone in when I wasn't in the office. I'm not at my desk every minute of the day. But while I have been here, I haven't seen anyone go in." His abruptness had rattled her at first but then she shifted to defensiveness at his accusatory tone. "Why? Is something missing? Maybe we didn't notice it when the police were first here."

Kyle realized he had come across more aggressively than he should have, but what he'd seen in Caleb's office had unnerved him. Most of the books that had been neatly stacked in the bookcases behind Caleb's desk, were now scattered on the floor as though someone had swept them off the shelves.

He started to explain, but stopped. Would this create more problems for him if the police were called back or a report was filed? He wanted to keep attention away from the office... and him... as much as possible.

"No, nothing's missing. There are books on the floor, but they must have just fallen off the shelf on their own. I'll put them back myself." The last thing he wanted was for Amber to see the full extent of the chaos. It was impossible that so many books could have fallen off the shelves without help. A shiver went up his spine. He hadn't ever believed in ghosts before, and he didn't want to begin now. He also didn't want to think about what other explanation there would be for how it happened. His body deflated as the shock of what he'd found retreated and remorse for how he'd handled it, settled in. "Sorry, Amber. I shouldn't have confronted you like that." He turned and walked back toward Caleb's office without waiting for her reply.

Amber watched his back as he retreated. It wasn't like Kyle to act that way. It might be grief that set him off, but her intuition wasn't buying that explanation. Something else was going on. He closed Caleb's door behind him and she could hear the sound of books being put on the shelves. It didn't stop after only one or two. Puzzled, she returned to the task she'd been doing before Kyle interrupted her but her subconscious filed the incident away.

Maybe there was an earthquake. Even Maine has them sometimes, or at least I think I've heard that. But wouldn't there be more than just the books on the floor? And nobody else's office had had anything disturbed. That point made a lot of sense but its logic wasn't what Kyle wanted to hear, even in his head. *Just put the books back and get what you came in for.* He found the file where it should be after he'd replaced the books and hurriedly walked to the door, shutting it behind him without looking back, his heart still racing in his chest. Once back in his office, he laid his hands palm down on his desk and closed his eyes. He took a deep breath through his nose, and slowly exhaled through his mouth. It took several rounds of breath before his heart returned to its normal rhythm and he was able to focus on his work again.

CHAPTER SEVENTEEN: EVA

"Did you hear the news about Kyle Mitchell?" Betty Jones hadn't even asked them for their orders yet when she sprang the question on Eva and Jim. They were in their usual booth at The Checkout Diner. Jim shook his head and shrugged his shoulders.

"I'm going to say no since I haven't heard any local news. What's up?" Eva asked.

Betty's face lit up, relishing that she was going to be the first to tell them. She finished pouring their water and set the pitcher on the table.

"Well, it seems that someone saw him leaving the office at the time Caleb was murdered. Daisy Bennett was walking on Lancaster Road and hadn't gotten to the office but she was close enough that she could see he was at the back door. He had his back to her, so she didn't think he saw her. It caught her attention because it looked like he was putting something into the door frame, but then the door opened and he went inside. That's where she usually turns around to go back to her house so that's what she did, and forgot all about it. She came in for lunch yesterday and we were talking about the fact that no one has been arrested for Caleb's murder and I mentioned that they'd gotten in through the back door. I thought her eyes were going to pop out of her head when I told her that. She got this funny look on her face so I asked her what was wrong and she told me what she'd seen, and asked me if it could have been Kyle who had broken in. We both thought it was strange he wouldn't have told the police he was the one who broke the door, but neither one of us could imagine he'd be the one who'd murdered Caleb. I told her she should report it to the police anyway. It could be important."

"That was the right thing to do, Betty," Jim told her and she beamed with pleasure at the praise. "Do you know if she's called them?"

"Yes. She did it right then. It took a couple minutes to get through to the right department, but a Detective Roberts took her information. Do you know him?"

"Actually, we both do," Eva replied, but didn't go on to explain her connection. Telling Betty she'd met them when the Cozy Quilts Club was investigating four other murders would be a huge mistake if she wanted to keep her involvement from becoming common knowledge. She'd let Betty assume she'd met them through Jim. Otherwise, the entire town of Glen Lake would know within a week or less.

Betty gave her a curious look but Eva kept her expression impassive and Jim intervened to take her focus away from Eva.

"I've worked with them on a couple cases. They're both stand-up guys and good at their jobs. They'll follow up on Daisy's report even if it turns out to be completely unrelated to Caleb's murder." He didn't bother to tell her he'd met them at around the same time as Eva had for the same reasons. That was a need-to-know piece of information that Betty didn't need to know.

"That's good. I hope it helps. Do you think Kyle could have done it?" she asked, conspiratorially, leaning down and keeping her voice low so the other diners wouldn't overhear her even though they weren't seated near Eva and Jim's booth.

"That would be terrible, wouldn't it?" Eva asked. She framed her response to intentionally keep from admitting she already knew he had.

"It sure would! Now, what can I get you folks?" Betty asked and the subject of Kyle Mitchell was closed in Betty's mind, for the moment.

Eva waited until they'd finished their meal and were on their way home before picking up the conversation again. Even keeping their voices quiet was too big a risk inside the diner. "Do you think Dennis and Phil will be able to arrest him now?"

"I think they can probably call him in for questioning as a person of interest. Sarah is going to have to prove he's the one who fabricated the emails between Caleb and Dylan. It still might not be enough to identify him as the killer, though. They'll need Kyle's confession to seal the case. He's the son of a lawyer and works in a law office. Even if they present all the evidence they have, he knows it's circumstantial. He'd have trouble claiming he was innocent of embezzling from the firm and even though that's motive, it doesn't directly tie him to the murder. They don't have the murder weapon or any forensics that connect him either."

Eva looked at the scenery passing by through the passenger window as she considered Jim's comments. The trees were all bare of leaves now and the sky was overcast with the threat of rain. It was late afternoon, almost twilight, although the clouds altering the daylight made it hard to distinguish the time. *It won't be long before it will be completely dark by this time of day.* That realization only added to her gloomy mood.

"Sarah's going to have to contact Caleb, isn't she?"

Jim glanced over at her and saw the concern on her face.

He didn't reply immediately. "It's made a difference before. It wasn't the only thing that helped close the other cases, but it gave Phil and Dennis information they needed to put everything together."

Eva sighed resignedly but didn't comment.

"She's worried about how to do that without letting more people know she talks to ghosts, isn't she?"

"Yes, that's exactly it. We'd already discussed this at one of our meetings. So far, we've been able to keep our methods secret for the most part. We all agreed we didn't want more people to know unless it was absolutely necessary. She would have to have help getting into Caleb's office. How do you think Dylan would react to that? He already knows about Jennifer's gift. Was he completely freaked out when she told him what she'd seen?"

Jim chuckled. "That would be an understatement. When she told him how he'd found the tablet and where, he had to believe her, though. It might take more convincing about Sarah. I've never actually seen her in action. Now that I think about it, neither have Phil or Dennis, have they?"

"No. The only ones outside the four of us who have, are Vivian Sullivan and Meghan Doherty. But Phil and Dennis know about it from the other cases we've worked on with them. I don't think Vivian and Meghan would have believed Sarah if they hadn't been there when she connected with Lily."

The month before, Meghan's roommate, Lily Sullivan, had been killed in their apartment. When she and Lily's sister, Vivian, had asked for Sarah's help, they had no idea it would include Sarah talking to Lily's ghost. The information Lily had provided helped in the investigation of her death. More importantly, it had healed the guilt Meghan and Vivian felt because they had believed Lily was involved in trafficking drugs. What they hadn't known until after her death, was that she was a confidential informant.

"I'll give this some thought about how to approach Dylan," Jim offered. He knew she was smiling even without looking.

"You're my hero."

"You may owe me a steak dinner after this," he teased.

"It's a price I'll happily pay if we can make this work." *Assuming I can convince Sarah, too,* she thought.

CHAPTER EIGHTEEN: KYLE

I t had only been three days since the odd events began, but Kyle felt like he hadn't slept in a week. He had dark circles under his eyes and all the color had drained from his skin giving it a gray pallor. When Erica asked if he was alright, he told her he was just worried about the bills. Fortunately, she believed him. After their conversation about their finances, it was a logical excuse. He briefly thought about telling her about the books in Caleb's office and his computer screen message and then dismissed it. It was just his imagination. If he could just get some sleep, this would all pass. In the meantime, a hot shower would help. Twenty minutes later, he did feel revived. The water had been as hot as he could stand it and even with the fan going, the bathroom mirror had steamed up. He brushed his teeth first thinking that might give it enough time to clear up before he had to shave, but it was still impossible to see his reflection. Taking the hand towel off the countertop, he wiped the mirror clean, humming softly to himself. He removed the shaver from its charging station and was about to begin shaving when he noticed something in the mirror. He let out a yelp and dropped the shaver into the sink bowl, still running. It made a buzzing sound as it continued to vibrate against the sink's surface but he was oblivious to it. He was focused on the reflection in the mirror. Not his face, but the translucent image of Caleb's face behind him slowly fading in and out as though he was trying to materialize. Caleb's lips were moving but no sound was coming out. Kyle didn't have to hear him to know what he was saying. It was the same thing he'd been hearing in his dreams every night. The same words that had appeared on his computer monitor.

"No! You're not real!" Kyle spat the words out. He squeezed his eyes shut, willing the vision to be gone before he opened them again. He remained motionless for a count of one hundred as his knuckles turned white from gripping the side of the vanity, and then slowly opened his eyes. Caleb's face was gone. *I told you, it's just your imagination.* Kyle wiped a shaky hand across his face before reaching for the shaver, still buzzing around in the sink. He clenched his hand tight to stop the shaking as he took a slow, steadying breath. This time, his hand was steady. He picked up the shaver and finished shaving his face. His hands may have become steady again, but the knot in his stomach was still there.

When he arrived at the office, Amber was in the break room. He thought about leaving before getting his coffee, but realized how awkward that would appear.

"Good morning, Kyle. Can I pour you a cup?" she asked, the carafe still in her hand. She looked up, and her smile turned into a look of concern. "Are you okay?"

"Just a little tired. I didn't sleep well." He smiled, hoping his excuse was believable and she would drop the line of questioning. "That coffee is just what I need."

She held his eyes a beat longer than necessary but didn't push the issue. "Here you go. If you decide to close your office door and take a nap, I'll make sure no one bothers you." Amber handed the mug to him, her lips curving up in a grin and gave him a wink. She took her own cup and walked back toward her office without waiting for him to reply.

As she was walking down the hall, she met Grace who was

headed to the break room. Turning around to make sure Kyle wasn't behind her, she whispered, "What's wrong with Kyle? He looks horrible."

"I haven't seen him today. What makes you think there's something wrong with him?" Grace asked.

"He's got purple circles under his eyes and I think he's lost weight. His face looks like it's…"

Grace put her hand on Amber's arm, stopping her in midsentence. "Good morning, Kyle!" she called out, her voice upbeat.

He gave her a mumbled good morning and walked up the stairway toward his office.

"I see what you mean," she said to Amber. "He's probably still grieving Caleb's death," is what she told Amber but inside she was thinking it was more. Her examination of the firm's books after seeing Sarah's report confirmed he was embezzling money through his fake software corporation. Dylan's suspicion that he was keeping a double set of books tied to their billing hours had been confirmed as well. He was inflating the invoice for the clients and withdrawing large amounts that were reported as petty cash and miscellaneous office supplies. This wasn't something Amber needed to know yet.

Amber nodded. "You're probably right. I told him he should shut his door and take a nap."

"Good advice. I need to go back to work now but let's have lunch later."

"Sounds good!"

Grace knocked on the open door of Dylan's office before going to her own office. When he looked up from his work and gestured for her to come in, she closed his door behind her.

"We need to talk."

2

"What's up?"

"Have you noticed how awful Kyle looks lately? I think he's on the verge of a nervous breakdown."

"I haven't seen him much this week. I think he's been avoiding me." Dylan was about to say *maybe he's having second thoughts about trying to incriminate me for Caleb's murder,* but caught himself. It wasn't time yet for Grace and Amber to know about that part of Kyle's deceptions.

"Do you think he knows we've found out he's embezzling?" Grace asked.

Dylan considered the possibility and then shook his head. "No, I don't think it's that. Sarah was very careful about how she looked into the finances so that she didn't leave any digital fingerprints for him to find. Plus, I don't think he's on her level of abilities in that regard."

There was a knock on the door and before Dylan could say come in, Kyle opened it and walked into the office, startling both Dylan and Grace.

"You two look like I caught you with your hands in the cookie jar," Kyle said. The words were spoken in jest but they both noticed his expression didn't reflect his attempt at humor.

Grace swallowed and took a deep breath to recover her composure.

"I had some questions for Dylan about your dad's estate," she said, looking Kyle straight in the eyes, hoping he wouldn't see through her lie.

"Anything I can answer for you?" Kyle asked.

"No, I think Dylan's answered them." She turned to Dylan and rose from her seat. "Thanks, Dylan. Will you be here later if I need anything else?"

"Yeah. I don't have to be in court today so I should be here."

She nodded and walked toward the door, giving Kyle a smile as she passed by him. Once she made it back to her office, she closed the door and sat at her desk. Her breath was shallow and her hands were shaking. She found her headphones and set her phone to an audio meditation. By the end, she had finally calmed herself.

"You look horrible. Are you okay, buddy?" Dylan asked when Kyle remained in his office once Grace had left. He'd been telling the truth when he'd said he hadn't noticed the change in Kyle's appearance, but now that he was here in front of him, the change was unmistakable.

"I'm not your buddy. Why does everyone keep asking me if I'm okay?" Kyle snarled.

"It looks like you haven't slept in a week. We're your friends. We're worried about you."

"Are you?" Kyle didn't attempt to hide the sarcasm in his voice. He walked out of Dylan's office without waiting for a reply. *They're plotting against you, Kyle. Watch your back.* The voice in his head wasn't Caleb's, but his paranoia edged up a notch.

You need to be careful, Dylan. Kyle's behavior had rattled him. He'd call the detectives later to get an update. He didn't want to take a chance on Kyle overhearing their conversation. If they didn't make an arrest soon, there was no telling what Kyle would do if he snapped.

3

He'd been too spooked to look for the tablet the day he'd seen the message on his monitor. Ever since then, though, Kyle had obsessed about checking Dylan's office despite the argument that if Dylan found it, he would have said something by now.

It was five-thirty before everyone left the building and Kyle's nerves were frayed as he locked the doors and walked into Dylan's office. He'd kept the gloves he'd worn when he first put it in the credenza in his office as insurance for this very occasion.

It's still there. He breathed a sigh of relief when he found it under the legal pads just where he'd put it. He was about to shut the drawer but felt a compulsion to turn it on. That's why he'd put on the gloves, so better to make sure the emails were still there otherwise he wouldn't be able to sleep tonight, wondering about them. He turned on the power and his shoulders relaxed when he scrolled through and everything was right where it should be. He returned it to its spot and closed the drawer. Now for the last step. It was time to call the detectives.

He'd already shut everything down for the night in his office but he had their cards in his wallet. The quiet of the office was creeping him out, and he wanted to leave. I can call them from the car. Chances are they're gone for the day, anyway. Half expecting to get voice mail, he jumped when he heard Dennis Smith's voice on the line.

"Oh. Detective Smith, this is Kyle Mitchell. I didn't think you'd still be in the office."

"You're in luck. I had some paperwork to turn in. How can I help you?"

"I had a chance to look in Dylan Johnson's office just before I called you and I found the tablet he used to send my father the emails. I didn't touch it, so my fingerprints won't be on it," he said, thinking that was a nice touch.

"That's good news, Mr. Mitchell. I'll need to get a court order before Detective Roberts and I can search his office, though. We want to make sure we've done everything by the book, especially when it's involving a lawyer. It's not likely that would happen until Monday, so you should expect us then. You don't think it's likely he would remove it over the weekend, do you?"

"No, probably not," Kyle said, feeling deflated after the anticipation of thinking the detectives would come immediately.

"In that case, have a good weekend, Mr. Mitchell. This will all be over soon."

I certainly hope so. I'm not sure how much more I can take.

"Mr. Mitchell?"

Kyle had drifted away for a second, lost in his thoughts.

"Yes, yes. I'm here. I'll see you Monday."

CHAPTER NINETEEN: AMBER AND GRACE

"*Mom*, you need to tell Noah to leave us alone!" Zoe Foster, Grace's eight-year-old daughter, stood in front of her mother with her hands on her hips and a look of extreme annoyance on her face.

Grace rolled her eyes at Amber who put her hand over her mouth to hide her smile. Their families were having an adult get-together and playdate for their children. Their husbands, Greg and Brad, were upstairs watching a football game.

"What's he doing?"

"Maddie and I are trying to play with our dolls and he and Ian keep bothering us," she said as though that was sufficient information for Grace to take action to remedy the situation.

"What's Ian doing?" Amber asked her daughter, Madison, when she came in to join them.

"He's making faces at us and repeating what we say," Maddie answered, as equally exasperated as Zoe.

"Can't you just ignore them? They're doing it because they know it's bothering you," Grace told Zoe.

Zoe huffed and scowled at Grace. "That's what you always say, but it doesn't work!" she whined.

Grace sighed. "Alright, I'm coming."

"Me, too," Amber said, following Grace into the playroom.

Maddie ran ahead of them to get there first. "You're in *trouble*," she told the boys, a smug look of satisfaction on her face.

"Maddie. That wasn't necessary," Amber chastised her. "If you all can't get along, we'll have to leave."

Maddie's face dropped and she looked down at her feet at hearing the threat.

"Yes, Mom."

"You don't want Ian to have to leave, do you?" Grace asked Noah.

"No," he replied, and stuck his lower lip out in a pout.

"Okay, then. Play nicely with each other!" Grace told them.

The children separated to opposite sides of the playroom where the girls went back to playing with their dolls and the boys went to the table set up for assembling the Lego pieces. Amber and Grace waited until they were sure the squabbling wouldn't resume as soon as they turned their backs.

"I give them half an hour," Amber speculated when they were back in their seats.

"We can hope," Grace agreed. She hesitated a moment debating with herself about whether to bring up Kyle.

"After you asked me about Kyle the other day, I talked to Dylan. We had the door closed so we wouldn't be overheard, but Kyle barged in. Well, he did knock but he didn't wait for Dylan to tell him it was okay to come in. He was acting really weird. Weird isn't quite the right word. Paranoid might be a better one. To be honest with you, he scared me, the way he was looking at us."

Amber's eyes got round and her lips parted slightly in shock.

"Do you think he's having a breakdown?" Grace asked.

"It's possible. He said he hadn't been sleeping lately and from the way he looks, that's easy to believe."

"I never expected this reaction from Kyle. It was clear that he and Caleb didn't have a great relationship so it surprises me that he's reacting to his death like this."

"Me, either. The way he yelled at me when he found the books on the floor in Caleb's office was completely out of character. He apologized, but I've been on guard ever since," Amber said.

"Do you think he would get physical?" Grace asked, concerned.

Amber thought for a moment. "If you'd asked me that before it happened, I would have said no way, but now I'm not so sure."

"Should we talk to Dylan about this? Maybe he could talk Kyle into taking some time off until he's not so wound up," Grace suggested.

"That's not a bad idea, as long as Kyle goes along with it. It could backfire if he thinks we're suggesting he's out of control."

"I don't think we have any other choice. We can't risk our safety or our clients. I'll talk to Dylan on Monday."

2

Grace called Dylan at home instead. After the last time, she didn't want to chance having Kyle coming in during their conversation.

"I understand completely. I'm not ashamed to admit the way he acted with us had me worried. I'll talk to Kyle. If he won't go along with it, then maybe I can have Erica convince him to take a break. And maybe see a grief counselor," he added as an afterthought.

"That's an excellent idea. Maybe you could talk to her first."

"I'll think about that. It could set him off even more if he thought I was going behind his back."

"That's a good point. Good luck. I don't envy you having that discussion," she said.

Dylan sat at his desk for several moments after they disconnected the call. "Might as well just get it over with," he said, resignedly. He set his shoulders and picked up his phone with a sense of dread at Kyle's reaction. His fears weren't unfounded. The suggestion was rebuffed and Dylan knew there was no point discussing it. He'd have to find a time to speak privately with Erica. In the meantime, he resolved to make sure he never left Amber and Grace alone in the office with Kyle.

CHAPTER TWENTY: SARAH

She'd made up her mind to do this, but now with her finger hovering over Jim's number on the screen of her phone, Sarah was wavering.

"What are you worried about, girl? You know Jim and if he isn't willing to get involved, he'll tell you. No harm, no foul. You'll figure out a different way to do it." She spoke the words out loud although only Max was there to hear her.

Max turned his head to the side first in one direction, and then the other and then gave a short bark as though to say, "Are you talking to me?"

She looked down at him and gave him a reassuring smile. "It's okay, buddy, I'm just working up my courage to make this call."

Woof!

"You're right. Just do it." She hit call and held her breath until Jim answered on the second ring.

"Sarah, you must be psychic, too. I was just about to call you."

"You were?" She scrunched her eyebrows together, confused.

"I have you on speaker and Eva is here with me. She told me last night about the discussion you all had at your Club meeting debating whether you should contact Caleb. I completely understand why you wouldn't want to expose yourself to more people about your ability, especially anyone outside your circle of friends and family."

"That's right. What made you bring that up, Eva?"

"Jim and I learned some news about Kyle Mitchell when we were at the Diner last night. Right now, all the evidence we have against him is circumstantial. We thought you might be able to learn more about what happened if you heard Caleb's side of the story. Jim thought if we got together with Dylan and Phil and Dennis, it would be easier to broach the subject and convince him we weren't pulling his leg. What do you think?"

"It's funny you should say that, because it's exactly why I was calling. I'm ready to do this. Go ahead and set it up and text me the details about when and where."

"That was easier than I expected," Eva said after she'd disconnected the call.

"Don't be too optimistic. That was only phase one."

2

The group was gathered in Eva's living room. With the exception of Dylan, they all understood why they were there. Jim had only told him they had a new witness statement they wanted to discuss with him as well as go over the status of the case.

"Have you spoken with Daisy Bennett?" Dylan asked the detectives when they'd finished giving their update.

"We did and we believe she is a credible witness. We went to the section of the road she described and it's entirely possible that Mr. Mitchell wasn't aware she was there."

"I brought a report Sarah and Grace Foster put together for you to look over which proves that Kyle was embezzling from the firm. It's a motive, but it's still not enough to present an airtight case to the DA's office. I think something is going on with him, though. He looks like he hasn't slept in a week and he made a scene a few days ago demanding to know who had been in Caleb's office and taken books off the bookcase and put them on the floor. Amber didn't go in but when he confronted her about it, there hadn't been enough time between when Kyle went in and then came out to have done it himself. Even if he did, she would have heard him doing it. I think he's beginning to lose it."

There was an awkward silence as Sarah, Eva, Jim, and the detectives all exchanged glances.

"Okay, what aren't you saying?" Dylan asked, his voice wary.

"I'll do it," Sarah told the others before turning to Dylan. "I'm going to tell you something that you will find difficult, or more likely, impossible, to believe but I'm telling the truth. You know about Jennifer's gift of psychometry. Mine is that I can speak with the dead. I don't think Kyle was lying. I'm convinced Caleb's presence is still here and he's the reason Kyle is falling apart. I'm hoping you will allow me to go into Caleb's office when everyone else has gone so I can try to make contact with him."

"Before you think we're all putting you on, even though I haven't seen Sarah do this, Eva has and she wouldn't lie to me about it," Jim said.

Phil Roberts cleared his throat and despite his embarrassment, which was evident on his face, stepped in. "Neither Dennis nor I have seen Sarah talking to ghosts either, but she's given us information she learned from speaking with the victims in other cases that has been instrumental in solving them. It may be asking you to suspend your disbelief, but what's the worst that would happen? If we can find out exactly what took place the night Caleb died, I hope you'll allow her to try."

Dylan looked from one to the other as though trying to

decide if they were punking him, but their serious expressions said otherwise.

"You can trust me when I say without a doubt I believe Sarah," Eva said. "I may be the only one in the room who has witnessed her in action and it was remarkable... no, life-changing is a better word. I didn't believe it before even though I can..." She was about to say *communicate with animals,* and caught herself. She heard Reuben meow and looked in his direction. If cats can have a smug expression, he did, and she knew he had guessed what she started to say. She scowled at him and heard Jim suppressing a chuckle by coughing. He knew what was going on, too, and she warned him with a glare that she didn't think it was funny. The exchanges had taken place in an instant, but she hurried on, trying not to let on that she was flustered, before the others took notice. "Well, I guess that's all I can say and I agree with Phil that the only thing that would convince you would be to let her try. It might give them just what they need to wrap up their investigation."

She felt Sarah's eyes on her and glanced over. Sarah gave her a discreet wink and a slight smile which put Eva at ease.

Dylan shrugged his shoulders and raised his hands palm up in resignation. "Okay, I'll get you into the office. Can you do this tomorrow night, around seven-ish?"

Sarah checked her calendar first and then replied that she could.

"Do I need to bring any candles or a Ouija board?" Dylan asked but when he saw the disapproving look on everyone's face, he quickly apologized. "Sorry, that was uncalled for. I'm obviously still having a hard time accepting this."

"It's why I don't make a habit of telling people and I'm asking you to keep this to yourself as well. I'm sure you don't need me to explain why," Sarah said.

Dylan nodded. "No, I get it. You're not a client, but I'll treat this as confidential information. How about we consider you a client for these purposes?" he suggested.

"What's your hourly rate?" Sarah asked, throwing Dylan off base. When she saw he wasn't sure if she was serious, she gave him a wide grin. "Gotcha."

3

They had agreed to keep the group small so it was just Dylan, Sarah, and Dennis Smith who met the next night at the Mitchell & Johnson law office. It was Sarah's first time, so Dylan gave her a tour of the rest of the offices before they went to Caleb's. His office door was closed as it had been ever since the morning his body had been discovered unless anyone needed access. Dylan turned on the light after opening the door and once the three of them stepped inside, he closed the door behind them. They all felt a discernible drop in temperature between the hallway and the office. Sarah walked around the room, stopping every so often to take a closer look at the furnishings before being drawn to the desk. She paused at the spot where Dennis had told her Caleb's body had been lying, but he stayed quiet.

"Why don't you have a seat?" she suggested as she became aware that the two men were still huddled at the doorway. "I can feel Caleb's presence so I'm going to attempt to make contact now. Even though I know he's here, it doesn't mean he'll speak with me, though."

They nodded their understanding.

"Mr. Mitchell, my name is Sarah Pascal." She looked in Dylan's direction. "Dylan agreed to let me come here to speak with you about the night you died. The other gentleman is Detective Smith. He's one of the homicide detectives assigned to your case. We think we know who killed you, but we'd like to hear your side of the events that took place that night." She shivered as the air around her became even colder, but there was no response. She remained still, giving Caleb time to decide if he wanted to speak and despite knowing his presence was nearby, began to doubt he would.

"It was an accident. Kyle didn't intend to kill me. I know that but I expected him to admit it instead of being dishonest. Even worse, he's trying to implicate Dylan as the one who did it." Only she could hear him, but the disappointment and anger in Caleb's voice came through loud and clear in her head.

"Would you tell me exactly what happened?"

Caleb described the argument they'd had and the surprise on Kyle's face after he'd thrown the paperweight, striking the fatal blow to Caleb's head. "That's how I knew he didn't mean for the paperweight to hit me. He threw it as he turned around without knowing I'd moved and was directly in its path."

Sarah told the men what she'd heard. "Did you find a glass paperweight at the scene? It's what Kyle threw at Caleb and was in the shape of a baseball," Sarah asked Dennis.

Sarah didn't need to repeat the question. Although Caleb couldn't respond directly to anyone other than Sarah, he was able to hear what everyone was saying. Before Dennis could reply, Caleb interrupted. "He took it with him. He picked it up with a paper towel and put it in his pocket."

"No..." Dennis began.

This time Sarah interrupted. "Caleb just told me Kyle took it with him. It's what hit Caleb on the head, killing him."

"The coroner's report makes sense now. He couldn't say definitively what object would have been the weapon."

"I think Kyle was embezzling from the firm," Caleb said.

"It wasn't a significant amount, but yes, he was." Sarah told Caleb what she and Grace had discovered. "I think he was only taking enough to keep himself above water at first, but he was living way beyond his means. He was in serious financial trouble and about to lose his home unless he could bring his payments up to date."

"That's Erica's fault," Caleb growled. "That woman always

had champagne tastes and Kyle never stood up to her. She knew exactly how to manipulate him and always got her way. That's why I refused to give him the loan. I knew it would just be a matter of time before he'd be back begging for more."

"Is there anything you'd like me to ask Caleb?" Sarah addressed the men.

"Does he know what Kyle intended to do with the paperweight? We haven't found it." Dennis asked.

"No, I only know he picked it up and put it in his pocket," Caleb answered without needing Sarah to ask him.

"No, he doesn't."

Dylan had remained mute all this time, too shocked to speak. Suddenly, he leaped out of his seat and walked briskly to the credenza. "I never even noticed it was missing," he said so quietly, Dennis and Sarah barely heard him. He turned around to face Sarah, his eyes like saucers. "You really are speaking to him."

Sarah nodded and grinned. "I am, but if you have something you'd like to ask, you should do it now. I don't know how long the connection will hold."

"Does Caleb want us to pursue filing charges for the embezzlement? The manslaughter charge won't be negotiable but we could work out a settlement with Kyle privately to repay what he's stolen."

Despite her impression of Caleb being inflexible, he surprised Sarah by considering Dylan's question instead of responding immediately in the affirmative.

"No, don't file charges. Let him use his inheritance to pay his bills. First to his creditors and then to the firm. He'll have to make amends for what he's done and there will be consequences, but he's my son..." Sarah heard the sadness and remorse in Caleb's voice. "I was always so hard on him. I just wanted him to be strong and responsible. Louise always told me I was too strict and Kyle needed to know I loved him. She told him that I did, but she said he should hear it from me. I wasn't raised that way. I didn't know how to show him that side of me. Even now, I've been unkind to him. I've been trying to force him to confess by terrifying him from this side of the veil. Maybe if I'd given him the loan just that once, the situation never would have gotten to this point..." He stopped speaking but Sarah sensed he wasn't finished and waited while he gathered his thoughts. "That's all. Tell Dylan what I said about taking it out of Kyle's inheritance and if that isn't sufficient, set up a payment schedule from his salary once he's able to work again. You don't need to repeat the rest. If Dylan can see it in his heart, I hope he'll let Kyle remain with the firm. It's time for me to go."

"I understand." She'd barely spoken the words when he disappeared. "He's gone, but he told me what he'd like you to do."

CHAPTER TWENTY-ONE: KYLE

1

"I think we've got everything we need to bring Kyle Mitchell in for questioning," Dennis told Phil Roberts. "After what Sarah Pascal was able to learn from Caleb Mitchell... I can't believe I just said that... or that I would ever believe someone who said they were talking to a ghost, but there we are," he said, shaking his head. "Anyway, with what she told Dylan and me, I think we can bluff Kyle into making a confession. He still thinks we have no idea what happened that night and are going after Dylan Johnson."

"What was it like?" Phil asked. Dennis had told him about Sarah's conversation but had recounted it with just the facts. "Did you see Caleb or could you hear him?"

"No, neither. It was like she was talking to air but I could feel something, or someone, was in the room. I can't explain it logically. I didn't get the impression she was making it up. It helped that I already knew she got information in other cases that turned out to be true. I'm not ashamed to admit that I could feel the hair on my arms rising and I got goosebumps. But if you ever told anyone else about it, I'd call you a liar." Dennis grinned but they both knew he was only half-joking.

"Don't worry. I'll take it to the grave, no pun intended."

"Just so you know, the next time she does this and one of us has to be with her, it's going to be your turn."

Phil raised his hands up in submission. "Okay, okay. If I'm lucky, there won't ever be another time. In the meantime, though, let's bring Kyle Mitchell in here and get him to confess so we can wrap this case up. Dylan Johnson knows what we're doing?"

"Yes, I told him last night that we are going to come to the office on Monday and *find*," he said using air quotes, "the tablet Kyle planted in Dylan's credenza. We'll make a show of it and read Dylan his rights. He's going to play the part and insist he's innocent. We agreed he wouldn't say anything to Amber Hayes or Grace Foster so their reactions will be unrehearsed. I'll call Kyle after we've taken Dylan and tell him we need him to come to give us an official statement about finding the emails to Caleb and the tablet in Dylan's office. We should probably split up to do the interrogation. It makes the most sense for me to question Kyle since I was the one with Sarah. Unless you think otherwise?"

"No, that makes perfect sense. If you need me, you can always call me in," Phil said.

2

"It's about time," Kyle muttered after disconnecting the call from Phil Roberts. Phil told him they were on their way to the office to retrieve the tablet in Dylan's credenza and would need Kyle to come to the station, too, to give them his statement. *Maybe this nightmare can finally be over.* He checked his emails and cleared his desk. Now that the moment was finally about to happen, he'd thought his anxiety would abate but the butterflies in his stomach and tightness in his chest were still there.

Twenty minutes later, he heard Amber greeting the detectives and debated going down to meet them but decided it would be best to wait for them to come to him. It didn't take long for his cell phone to announce an incoming text from Amber.

> The police are here with a search warrant for Dylan's office. They're in his office now. Should you come down?

A smile crossed his face. *It's happening!*

> I'll be right down.

He thought about going down the back stairway, which was closer, but wanted to make sure Amber saw him. When he reached the bottom of the stairs, she was standing in the hallway looking toward Dylan's office, an expression of bewilderment and shock on her face. She jumped when he put his hand on her shoulder.

"Sorry, didn't mean to startle you. Do you know what they're looking for?" he asked.

"No idea. They wouldn't tell me.'

Just then Dylan came out of his office, his eyebrows furrowed and when he glanced their way, they could see his anger. Kyle had to control himself not to gloat and show concern instead. Dylan walked rapidly toward them, his hands clenched, and Kyle's smugness faded away.

"What's going on, Dylan?" Amber asked.

"They claim someone gave them a tip that I have evidence in my office relating to Caleb's murder."

He gave Kyle a seething glance, making him step back involuntarily. Before Kyle could speak, the detectives came out of Dylan's office with the tablet in an evidence bag and approached the group still huddled in the hallway.

"Mr. Johnson, you're going to need to come with us to the station," Phil Roberts told him and read him his Miranda rights.

"Are you placing me under arrest?" Dylan replied, challenging the detective.

"For now, you're only a person of interest but we're Mirandizing you as a formality. As a lawyer, I'm sure you understand why we would do that. If we find what we've been told to expect on this tablet, that could change," Dennis Smith replied. "It would be best if you come to the station to give us your side."

"There is no side. I've never seen that before. Someone had to have planted it in my office."

"Mr. Johnson, it would be much easier for all of us if you come voluntarily," Phil said.

Dylan hesitated and Kyle thought he might push the issue and make them arrest him. The tension in the room was electric. Amber's head was swiveling between the detectives and Dylan as she followed their interaction, her eyes as big as saucers and Kyle thought she was holding her breath. That was confirmed when he heard her exhale when Dylan broke the silence.

"Fine. I'll go with you. I'm going to get my overcoat from the closet if that's alright with you," he said, a slight tinge of sarcasm in his tone. He pointed toward the closet door behind the detectives.

"Of course," Roberts said.

The detectives waited as Dylan retrieved his coat and the three of them exited the building with Dylan in the lead and the detectives following behind.

"How did I do?" Dylan asked when they were all in the car and safely out of earshot.

Dennis turned to face Dylan who was sitting in the back seat. Phil was driving but gave him a smile in the rearview mirror.

"You did great!" Dennis said. "It was a good move not to clue in Ms. Hayes or Ms. Foster."

"I'm going to have to apologize to them later but having Kyle see their reactions made it seem real. Once they know why I did it, they'll forgive me. I'm not so sure about Kyle, though."

"Speaking of which, I'll give him a call now and invite him down to the station. I don't think he suspects a thing."

———

"I can't believe that just happened," Amber said, softly.

The front door opened again and Grace walked in, a puzzled look on her face.

"Why is Dylan going with the detectives?" she asked.

"They found a tablet in his office that they said is connected to Caleb's murder. They're taking him to the police station for questioning," Kyle said, struggling to keep from sounding happy about the turn of events.

"*What?!*" Grace exclaimed and turned back toward the doorway, as though she was going to see some explanation for her confusion outside despite the door being closed.

Kyle's phone rang and he removed it from his pocket.

"Yes, of course, I'll come right down," he said, and disconnected the call. "That was Detective Smith. He wants me to come to the station, too. He has some questions he thinks I can answer," he explained for Amber and Grace's benefit. "I'll let you know what's happening as soon as I can. Amber, you'll need to cancel Dylan's appointments for the rest of the day. Just say an emergency has come up and you'll have to call them back to reschedule when you have more information."

Amber only nodded her head, too stunned to say more.

"What in the world is going on?" Grace asked when Kyle had left.

"I don't know, but it doesn't sound good, whatever it is." She went to her office to begin making her calls and Grace climbed the stairs to her own office.

Grace's initial shock at what had just happened was receding and her logical mind was back in control. Her first thought was *Did Kyle find out we know about the embezzlement?* Her next thought was *Is he setting Dylan up and will I be next?* Her stomach felt queasy at the possible repercussions. All she could do for now, though, was wait.

3

"Thank you for coming, Mr. Mitchell. Detective Roberts is with Mr. Johnson so I'll take your statement if you'll just follow me," Dennis greeted Kyle.

Kyle followed him to a small conference room. It was only big enough for a kitchen size table with two chairs on either side. There was a closed manilla file folder and legal pad on the table as well as what looked like a recording device. Kyle's stomach lurched as he saw the tablet in its evidence bag on the table as well. He glanced at the mirror on the wall wondering if it was a two-way mirror like in the movies and on TV.

Dennis gestured for Kyle to take a seat facing the mirror and Kyle's anxiety ratcheted up a notch. He took a slow breath through his nose to calm himself without being obvious about it. *You're here to tell them about the tablet and emails just like you did when you first reported them. They must believe Dylan did it if they brought him in for questioning. No need to be worried.*

Dennis took a pen out of the inside pocket of his suit jacket, and slid the legal pad closer but placed the pen on top of the pad instead of holding it in his hand to write.

"Do you mind if I record our conversation? It carries more

weight with a jury if they can hear what you had to say instead of just having the written statement."

"Oh, sure. No problem," Kyle answered, willing himself to stay calm and keep his face expressionless.

Dennis turned on the recorder and stated the date and their names.

"Now, for the record, Mr. Mitchell, would you please tell me about the emails you found between your father, Caleb Mitchell, and his law partner, Dylan Johnson?"

The detective remained impassive as Kyle repeated the story he'd fabricated.

"This is the tablet we recovered earlier today from Mr. Johnson's office. Can you tell me if this is the same tablet you discovered on November sixth?" Dennis slid it toward Kyle so he could take a better look.

"Is it okay if I pick it up?"

"As long as you don't open the evidence bag," Dennis said.

Kyle took the tablet and turned it over so he could examine both sides.

"It appears to be the same one."

Dennis opened the folder and removed the top sheet.

"We were able to track the store where it was sold through the serial number. It was purchased with cash about a week before you found it in Mr. Johnson's office. This is a problem because the emails you also found are dated prior to that. Can you explain that Mr. Mitchell?"

Kyle's stomach clenched even tighter and he felt a light sheen of sweat on his forehead.

"No, I can't explain it. Couldn't Dylan have transferred them from another computer?"

"Well, here's another problem. The email that he supposedly used to create the emails also wasn't opened until after the tablet was purchased. We were able to get that information from the service provider."

Kyle suddenly had a realization about Dennis's questions.

"How could you possibly have done all that? You've only had the tablet less than an hour."

"Actually, Mr. Mitchell, we've known about the tablet for much longer. Long enough for us to obtain this information. We also have a photo of you in the store where the tablet was purchased. It was paid for in cash but with the time stamp on the surveillance video and the sale receipt, we believe you are the one who purchased it."

Kyle's face blanched. "It's a coincidence. I was there to buy my son a tablet for school."

"We both know that isn't true, Mr. Mitchell, but we'll leave that for now." Dennis removed several more papers from the folder. "This is a report proving that you've been stealing from your father's law firm for the past year. You're in a lot of financial trouble, Mr. Mitchell." Dennis slid the papers over to Kyle.

Kyle sat with his hands in his lap, staring at the papers, while Dennis waited for him to make a move. At last, he raised his hands, which Dennis saw were shaking slightly, and drew the papers closer. It was all there. The corporation he'd created, the billing, the bank account he'd set up.

"I'm being set up. Dylan did this, didn't he?" Kyle raised his eyes to meet Dennis's.

Dennis ignored the question.

"We have a witness who saw you breaking into the back door of the office that night. She can place you at the office at the time of death."

"That's impossible. When I left my father was alive." His voice came out in a croak and now his chest was as tight as his stomach. He began to take shallow breaths and caught himself. *Slow breaths, Kyle. Slowly through your nose.*

"What did you do with the paperweight, Kyle?"

Kyle's mouth dropped open and his eyes widened. "How… who told you…" He shook his head as though trying to clear it. "What are you talking about? What paperweight?"

"The one that's missing from your father's credenza."

Dennis and Kyle stared at each other, waiting for the other to be the first to speak. Dennis knew he'd shaken Kyle, but he had to get a confession. Time to try another approach.

"Listen, we've heard how Caleb was toward you. He wasn't exactly your warm, fuzzy type of father. So, what happened? You went to him to ask for a loan and he turned you down? You must be pretty desperate from what I've seen of the bills that are overdue and your house is close to going into foreclosure. He made you angry, right? You were just asking for a loan, not a gift. It's the least he could do for you and your family. Did that make you angry, Kyle? Angry enough to grab the paperweight and throw it?"

Kyle was visibly shaken and the sheen of perspiration on his forehead had turned into a line of sweat trickling down his temple. *How could he know this? No one else was in the office. He'd checked..*

"It was an accident. You didn't mean to kill him. You probably didn't even intend to hit him. You had your back to him and when you turned around, he'd moved. If you'd known he was there, you would never have thrown that paperweight no matter how angry you were. Am I getting warm, Kyle?"

The stress he'd been under finally broke him. "I smashed it. I smashed it into a million pieces and threw it in the trash. There. Is that what you wanted to hear?" he said, his voice raised and his face contorted in anger. He turned his head away and his face turned white as he faced the two-way mirror.

"I'm so sorry, Dad. I didn't mean to hit you. I was aiming for the wall behind you. Are you happy now? I've admitted it. Will you please just leave me alone?"

Kyle was staring at the mirror as though he was seeing and speaking to Caleb. Although he knew nothing would be there, Dennis turned around to look at the mirror. After being witness to Sarah's connection to Caleb, though, a part of him wouldn't have been surprised to see his face and it was with relief he saw only Kyle's.

Kyle began to weep until sobs were wracking his chest and he covered his face with his hands. Dennis waited until, at last, Kyle regained control of his emotions and wiped his eyes with the heels of his hands.

"You're right, I didn't mean to kill him. It happened pretty much like you said, but how did you know?"

"Educated guess. Kyle Mitchell, you're under arrest for the murder of Caleb Mitchell."

EPILOGUE

"I can't believe it's only been a week since Kyle was arrested," Eva said.

The Club was gathered for their last meeting of the month and the hot topic for the evening was Kyle Mitchell. Dennis and Phil had told them how Kyle was arrested and arraigned, but on a charge of manslaughter instead of homicide. He would be brought to trial in time, but had been released on bail.

"I was at The Checkout for take-out a couple nights ago and Betty told me that Erica has taken the kids and moved in with her parents down in Kittery," Annalise said.

"It doesn't surprise me. I don't think she could handle the embarrassment of facing people in Glen Lake after what's happened," Jennifer said.

"Dylan told Chris that Kyle has moved into his father's house for now and is going to put their house on the market. They're trying to work out a plea deal for him. Kyle is going to plead guilty to a charge of manslaughter to avoid a trial. I think he mentioned working with Danielle Larson to see if they would agree to placing Kyle under house arrest instead of prison."

"That's what he told me, too," Sarah joined in. "He's going to honor Caleb's request not to bring charges against Kyle for the funds he'd embezzled from the firm. He'll have to repay the money he stole, of course. What did surprise me more is that he's allowing Kyle to continue in his job at the firm but he no longer has any access to the firm's bank accounts. I don't think I could have been that forgiving if I'd been in his position."

"He might not have if Caleb hadn't asked him to keep him on," Eva said.

"So, I was right about Caleb haunting Kyle," Annalise said.

"Yes. Caleb admitted to me what he'd been doing," Sarah replied.

"It's so sad. So many lives affected because of stubbornness and being unwilling to bend," Eva said, shaking her head.

"Caleb had named Peyton and Zach as the alternate beneficiaries of the life insurance policy. Kyle can't collect the proceeds because he's the one who is responsible for Caleb's death. It will be in a trust, so they'll be taken care of," Jennifer said. "Dylan was named as the trustee so Erica won't have access to it."

Who rained on your parade? Reuben asked. He'd come into the dining room to join them at the tail end of their conversation and the mood was still somber.

"Just reflecting on an unfortunate set of circumstances, Reuben. But he's right, ladies. No more rain on this parade. It's time for our show and tell. And let me tell you this! I don't think I'll be making another coin quilt anytime soon. It was great to use up some of my scraps but getting all the seams to match! Ai yi yi. It turned out okay but it's mostly why I decided to switch from making a throw quilt to a two-person picnic blanket size. Let's go take a look at how we did."

"I'm glad I only did a table runner for the same reason," Sarah agreed once they'd gathered in Eva's sewing room. "That was my original plan since I don't have a lot of fabric in my stash yet, but by the time I'd finished the runner, I was relieved I don't!"

That got a sympathetic chuckle from the others.

"Call me crazy, but I enjoyed it. It was a personal challenge to nest all the seams and I had a sense of achievement when a row turned out as close to perfect as I could get," Annalise said.

"You're crazy!" Jennifer teased. "I put a sash in between my rows because I thought it would be easier to avoid matching the seams. Unfortunately, my perfectionism got in the way when I was sewing everything together and the rows didn't line up. It would have been better if I'd just done it like the rest of you."

"It turned out great, Jen. We're our worst critics and unless you pointed it out, I'm not seeing what you are."

"That's the problem, though, Eva. *I* see it every time I look at the quilt."

"Finished is better than perfect," Annalise reminded Jennifer.

"You're right. And someday I might actually believe that," Jennifer said with a smile.

"I'm not sure how much I'll actually use mine. I'd told Jim that it was a picnic blanket and suggested we could use it next summer. He gave me a side-eye and told me his days of sitting on the ground to eat his meals were over."

The honeymoon must be over, Reuben said drily.

"You're right about that, Reuben, but I'm okay with how we're getting along now," Eva said and explained what Reuben had said.

"It would be a shame not to use the blanket after all the work you put into it. I'd be happy to go on picnics with you," Annalise offered.

That made Eva beam. "You're on. I've been wanting to go to the Coast. We'll have to make sure to do that. Or any other place you suggest," she added, realizing Annalise might have her own ideas about places to go. "Well, that's another one in the can. I think that's the right expression. Maybe one of these days we'll have a quilt project without a murder to solve, too," Eva said.

They all looked from one to the other.

"I wouldn't bet on it," Annalise said and winked.

———

If you enjoyed this book, I hope you will consider leaving a review. Even just a star review would be most appreciated. You can find the Amazon page to leave a review here:

https://Amazon.com/review/create-review?&asin=B0DGY84XWW

———

Don't miss the next adventure of the Cozy Quilts Club, *The Christmas Craft Fair Caper,* coming soon.

ACKNOWLEDGMENTS

Writing a book can be a solitary process but as an indie writer/publisher, the work doesn't end once the last page is written. The proverb it takes a village is a more accurate description of what it takes to go from that first word on the blank page to the finished product. My village included my wonderful beta readers and editors whose feedback helped turn my rough draft into the final version presented on the previous pages. Without my Wily Writers village, my writing career would have ended several books ago. It has been their selfless sharing of information, encouragement, and support which has kept me going in my moments of self-doubt. And, of course, thank you to all of the readers who have bought my books and supported my career. I couldn't have done it without all of you; my village.

ALSO BY MARSHA DEFILIPPO

Arizona Dreams

Deja vu Dreams

Disillusioned Dreams

A Cozy Quilts Club Mystery series

Follow the Crumbs

Finding the Treasure

Summer's End

Caught in a Spider's Web

Pulling Out the Hidden Stitches

(Click to download this free short story tie-in or use the QR code)

ABOUT THE AUTHOR

After retiring from her day job of nearly 33 years, Marsha DeFilippo has embarked on a new career of writing books. She is also a quilter and lifelong avid crafter who has yet to try a craft she doesn't like. She spends her winters in Arizona and the remainder of the year in Maine.

For more information, please visit my website:
marsha defilippo.com

To get the latest information on new releases, excerpts and more, be sure to sign up for Marsha's newsletter.
https://marshadefilippo.com/newsletter

Made in United States
Cleveland, OH
04 February 2025

14058929R00090